CLAIMING HIS ONE-NIGHT BABY

BY

MICHELLE SMART

MILLS
BOON®

First published in Great Britain 2017
By Mills & Boon, an imprint of HarperCollins*Publishers*
1 London Bridge Street, London, SE1 9GF

Large Print edition 2018

© 2017 Michelle Smart

ISBN: 978-0-263-07322-5

MIX
Paper from
responsible sources
FSC
www.fsc.org   FSC® C007454

This book is produced from independently certified
FSC™ paper to ensure responsible forest management. For
more information visit www.harpercollins.co.uk/green.

Printed and bound in Great Britain
by CPI Group (UK) Ltd, Croydon, CR0 4YY

For Adam xxx

CHAPTER ONE

JAW CLENCHED, HIS heart pounding an irregular beat in his chest, Matteo Manaserro watched the coffin being lowered into the consecrated ground of Castello Miniato's private cemetery.

Surrounding the open earth stood hundreds of Pieta Pellegrini's loved ones, friends, family, colleagues, even some heads of state, with their security details standing back at a discreet distance, all there to say a final goodbye to a man who had been respected the world over for his philanthropic endeavours.

Vanessa Pellegrini, Pieta's mother, who had buried her husband, Fabio, in the adjoining plot only a year ago, stepped forward, supported by her daughter Francesca. Both women clutched red roses. Francesca turned around to extend a hand to Natasha, Pieta's widow, who was staring blankly at the wooden box like an ashen-faced statue. The breeze that had filled the early-autumn air had dropped, magnifying the statue effect. Not a single strand of her tumbling honey-blonde hair moved.

She lifted her dry eyes and blinked, the motion seeming to clear her thoughts as she grabbed Francesca's hand and joined the sobbing women.

Together, the three Pellegrini women threw their roses onto the coffin.

Matteo forced stale air from his lungs and focused his attention anywhere but on the widow.

This was a day to say goodbye, to mourn and then celebrate a man who deserved to be mourned and celebrated. This was not a day to stare at the widow and think how beautiful she looked even in grief. Or think how badly he wanted to take hold of her shoulders and…

Daniele, Pieta's brother, shifted beside him. It was their turn.

Goodbye, Pieta, my cousin, my friend. Thank you for everything. I will miss you.

Once the immediate family—in which Matteo was included—had thrown their roses on the coffin, it was time for the other mourners to follow suit.

Striving to keep his features neutral, he watched his parents step forward to pay their last respects to their nephew. They didn't look at him, their son, but he knew his father sensed him watching.

Matteo hadn't exchanged a word with them since he'd legally changed his surname five years ago in the weeks that had followed the death of his own brother.

So much death.

So many funerals.

So much grief.

Too much pain.

When the burial was over and the priest led the mourners into the *castello* for the wake, Matteo hung back to visit a grave on the next row.

The marble headstone had a simple etching.

Roberto Pellegrini
Beloved son

No mention of him being a beloved brother.

Generations of Pellegrinis and their descendants were buried here, going back six centuries. At twenty-eight, Roberto was the youngest to have been buried in fifty years.

Matteo crouched down and touched the head-stone. 'Hello, Roberto. Sorry I haven't visited you in a while. I've been busy.' He laughed harshly. In the five years since his brother's death he'd visited the grave only a handful of times. Not a day passed when he didn't think of him. Not an hour passed when he didn't feel the loss.

'Listen to me justifying myself. Again. You know I hate to see you here. I love you and I miss you. I just wanted you to know that.'

Blinking back moistness from his eyes, his heart aching, his head pounding, Matteo dragged himself to the *castello* to join the others.

A huge bar had been set up in the state room for the wake. Matteo had booked himself into a hotel in Pisa for the next couple of days but fig-ured one small glass of bourbon wouldn't put him over the limit. His hotel room had a fully stocked minibar for him to drink dry when he got there. He would stay as long as was decent then leave.

He'd taken only a sip of his drink when Fran-cesca appeared at his side.

He embraced her tightly. 'How are you holding up?' He'd been thirteen when his uncle Fabio and his wife, Vanessa, had taken him into their home. Francesca had been a baby. He'd been there when she'd taken her first steps, been in the audience for her first school music recital—she'd murdered the trumpet—and had beamed with the pride of a big brother only a few months ago at her graduation.

She shrugged and rubbed his arm. 'I need you to come with me. There's something we need to discuss.'

Following her up a cold corridor—the ancient *castello* needed a fortune's worth of modernisation—they entered Fabio Pellegrini's old office, which, from the musty smell, hadn't been used since the motor neurone disease that eventually killed him had really taken its hold on him.

A moment later Daniele appeared at the door with Natasha right behind him.

Startled blue eyes found his and quickly looked away as Francesca closed the door and indicated they should all sit round the oval table.

Matteo inhaled deeply and swore to himself.

This was the last thing he needed, to be stuck in close confines with *her*, the woman who had played him like a violin, letting him believe she had genuine feelings for him and could see a future for them, when all along she'd been playing his cousin too.

It seemed she had been with him every minute of that day, always in the periphery of his vision even when he'd blinked her away. Now she sat opposite him, close enough that if he were to reach over the table he would be able to stroke her deceitful face.

She shouldn't be wearing black. She should be wearing scarlet.

He despised that she was still the most beautiful woman he'd ever seen and that the years had only added to it.

He studied the vivid blue eyes that looked everywhere but at him. He studied the classically oval face with its creamy complexion, usually golden but today ashen, searching for flaws. Her nose was slightly too long, her lips too wide, but instead of being imperfections they added character to the face he'd once dreamed of waking up to.

And now?

Now he despised the very air she breathed.

'To summarise, I'll take care of the legal side, Daniele takes care of the construction and Matteo takes care of the medical side. What about you, Natasha? Do you want to handle publicity for it?'

Francesca's words penetrated Natasha's ears but it took a couple of beats longer for her brain to decipher them.

She'd struggled to pay attention throughout the meeting Francesca had called, the outbursts of temper between Daniele and Francesca being the only thing that had kept her even vaguely alert.

'I can do that,' she whispered, swallowing back the hysteria clamouring in her stomach.

Ignore Matteo and keep it together, she told herself in desperation.

God, she didn't know anything about publicity.

She knew Francesca thought she was doing the right thing, inviting her to this meeting of siblings—and the Pellegrinis considered their cousin Matteo to be a sibling—and that Francesca assumed she would want to be involved.

Any decent, loving widow would want to be involved in building a memorial to their beloved husband.

And she *did* want to be involved. For all his terrible failings as a husband, Pieta had been a true, dedicated humanitarian. He'd formed his own foundation a decade ago to build in areas hit by natural disasters; schools, homes, hospitals, whatever was needed. The Caribbean island of Caballeros had been hit by the worst hurricane on record the week before he'd died, wrecking the majority of the island's medical facilities. Pieta had immediately known he would build a hospital there but before his own plans for it had fully formed his own tragedy had struck and he'd been killed in a helicopter crash.

He deserved to have this memorial. The suffering people of Caballeros deserved to benefit from the hospital Francesca would steamroller into building for them.

So Natasha had striven to pay attention, not wanting to let down the loving Pellegrini siblings who'd been a part of her life for as long as she could remember, since her father and Fabio had been old school friends. She'd never had siblings of her own and as soon as it had been announced she'd be marrying into the family the closeness had grown, even during the six long years of their engagement.

If only Matteo weren't there she'd have been better able to concentrate.

There had not been one occasion in his presence in the past seven years where she hadn't felt the weight of his animosity. Polite and amiable enough that no one could see the depths of his loathing, whenever their eyes met it was akin to being stared at by Lucifer, her soul scorched by the burn of the hatred firing from green eyes that had once looked at her with only tenderness.

She could feel it now, digging into her skin like needles.

How could Francesca and Daniele not feel it too? How did it not infuse the whole atmosphere?

A part of her understood why he despised her as he did and, God knew, she'd tried to apologise for it, but it had been seven years. So much had changed in that time. She'd changed. He'd changed too, turning his back on the reconstructive surgery he'd worked so hard to specialise in and instead going the vanity surgery route. With his twenty-eight clinics worldwide and the patent on a skincare range he'd personally developed that actually worked in reducing scars and the signs of aging, he'd gone from being a dedicated professional surgeon to an entrepreneur who fitted surgery in when he had the time. Matteo had amassed a fortune that rivalled the entire Pellegrini estate and Pieta's personally accrued wealth put together.

He'd even changed his surname.

He'd become famous with it. Tall with dark good looks, olive skin, strong jaw and black curly hair that he'd recently had cropped short, it had been inevitable. 'Dr Dishy' the tabloids called him. It seemed she could barely pass a newsagent or log on to the internet without seeing his seductive face blazing out at her, normally with some identikit lingerie model or other draped on his arm.

Today his usual arrogance had deserted him.

Even with the laser burn of his loathing infecting her, she could feel his anguish.

Pieta had been more than a cousin and surrogate sibling. He'd been Matteo's closest friend.

Her heart wanted to weep for him.

Her heart wanted to weep for all of them.

Matteo pulled his car up by the kerb and turned off the engine. The grand town house he'd parked opposite from stood in darkness.

Slumping forward over the wheel, he closed his eyes.

What was he even doing here?

He should be in his hotel room, drinking the minibar dry. He'd made that arrangement assuming Natasha would be staying in the *castello* with the rest of the family. He hadn't slept under the same roof as her since she'd accepted Pieta's proposal.

But she hadn't stayed. A couple of hours after their meeting to discuss the memorial for Pieta she had made the rounds to embrace everyone goodbye. Everyone except him. By unspoken agreement—unspoken because he hadn't exchanged more than a handful of words with her in seven years—he'd kept a great enough physical distance between them that no one would notice they failed to say goodbye to each other.

He put his head back and breathed deeply, willing his heart to stop this irregular rhythm.

What the hell was wrong with him? Why was it today of all days that he couldn't shake her from his mind? Why today, when he was mourning his best friend and cousin, had the old memories returned to haunt him?

He could see it so vividly, leaving his room in the *castello* to head outside to join the rest of his family in the marquee for his aunt and uncle's thirtieth wedding anniversary party. Natasha had left the room she'd been sharing with Francesca just a short way up the corridor from his at the same time. His heart had skipped to see her and he'd been ecstatic to see the necklace he'd sent for her eighteenth birthday there around her slender neck. He'd been disappointed not to make it to England for her party but he'd been a resident doctor at a hospital in Florida close to where he'd been to medical school. An emergency had cropped up at the end of his shift, a major car crash with multiple casualties that had resulted in all hands on deck. By the time they'd patched up the last casualty he'd missed his flight.

He'd been taking things slowly with her, waiting for her to turn eighteen before making a physical move. And then, in that cold *castello* corridor, Natasha in an electric-blue dress, the epitome of a chic, elegant woman, he'd realised he didn't have to back off any more.

All the letters and late-night calls they'd been exchanging for months, the dreams and hopes for the future they'd shared, had all been leading to this, this moment, this time. It was time for their future to begin right then and he'd fingered that necklace before taking her face in his hands and kissing her for the very first time.

It had been the sweetest, headiest kiss he'd ever experienced in his then twenty-eight years, interrupted only by Francesca steamrolling from her room and clattering up the corridor to join them. If she'd been three seconds earlier she would have found them together.

Three seconds.

What would she have done, he wondered, if she had caught them in that clinch?

Because only two hours later Pieta had got to his feet and, in front of the three hundred guests, had asked Natasha to marry him. And she'd said yes.

Matteo rubbed his eyes as if the motion could rub the memories away.

He shouldn't be thinking of all this now.

Why had he even come here, to the house she had shared with Pieta?

A light came on upstairs.

Had she just woken? Or had she been in the darkness all this time?

And was Francesca right to be worried about her?

Francesca had cornered him as he'd been making his own escape from the wake and asked him to keep an eye on Natasha while she, Francesca, was in Caballeros. She was worried about her, said she'd become a lost, mute ghost.

Although Natasha and Pieta had only been married for a year, they'd been together for seven years. She might be a gold-digging, heartless bitch but surely in that time she must have developed some feelings for him.

He'd wanted her feelings for Pieta to be genuine, for his cousin's sake. But how could they have been when she'd been seeing them both behind each other's backs?

Other than the few social family occasions he'd been unable to get out of, he'd cut her out of his life completely. He'd blocked her number, deleted every email and text message they'd exchanged and burned all her old-fashioned handwritten letters. The times he'd felt obliged to be in her presence he'd perfected the art of subtly blanking her in a way that didn't draw attention to anyone but *her*.

He should have just said no to Francesca. Lied and said he was returning home to Miami earlier than planned.

Instead he'd nodded curtly and promised to drop round if he had five minutes over the next couple of days.

So why had he driven here when he'd left the *castello* fully intending to drive straight to the hotel?

* * *

Natasha pushed Pieta's study door open and swallowed hard before stepping into it. After a moment she switched the light on. After going from room to room in complete darkness, in the house that had been her home for a year, her eyes took a few moments to adjust to the brightness.

She didn't know what she was looking for or what she was doing. She didn't know anything. She was lost. Alone.

She'd stayed at the wake as long as had been decently possible but all the consolation from the other mourners had become too much. Seeing Matteo everywhere she'd looked had been just as hard. Harder. Her mother pulling her to one side to ask if there was a chance she could be pregnant had been the final straw.

She'd had to get out before she'd screamed the *castello* down and her tongue ran away with itself before she could pull it back.

The rest of the Pellegrinis were staying at the *castello* and with sympathetic but concerned eyes had accepted her explanation that she wanted to be on her own.

At her insistence, the household staff had all stayed at the wake.

This was the first time she'd been alone in the house since she'd received the terrible news.

Feeling like an intruder in the room that had been her husband's domain, she cast her gaze over the walls thick with the books he'd read. A stack of files he'd brought home to work on, either from his law firm or the foundation he'd been so proud of, lay on his desk. Next to it sat the thick leather-bound tome on Stanley and Livingstone she'd bought him for his recent birthday. A bookmark poked out a third of the way through it.

Her throat closing tightly, she picked the book up and hugged it to her chest then with a wail that seemed to come from nowhere sank to the floor and sobbed for the man who had lied to her and everyone else for years, but who had done so much good in the world.

Pieta would never finish this book. He would never see the hospital his siblings would build in his memory. He would never take delivery of the new car he'd ordered only the day before he'd died.

He would never have the chance to tell his family the truth about who he'd really been.

'Oh, Pieta,' she whispered between the tears. 'Wherever you are, I hope you're finally at peace with yourself.'

The sound of the doorbell rang out.

She rolled into a ball and covered her ears.

The caller was insistent, pressing the doorbell intermittently until she could ignore it no longer. Wiping the tears away, she dragged herself up from the study floor and went down the stairs, clinging to the bannister for support, mentally preparing what she would say to get rid of her unexpected visitor.

Please don't be my parents. Don't be my parents. Don't be my parents.

Bracing herself, she unlocked the door and opened it a crack to peer through.

Certain she must be hallucinating, she pulled the door wider.

Her heart seemed to stop then kick back to life with a roar.

Matteo stood there, shining like an apparition under the brilliance of the moon.

He'd removed his black tie, his white shirt open at the throat, bleakness in his eyes, his jaw clenched, breathing heavily.

Their eyes met.

Neither of them spoke.

Something erupted in her chest, gripping her so tightly her lungs closed.

Time came to a standstill.

There they stood for the longest time, speaking only with their eyes. She read a hundred things in his; variations of pain, misery, anger and something else, something she hadn't seen since the beat before he'd taken her into his arms for the only kiss they had ever shared seven years ago.

This was the first time she'd seen him alone since that kiss.

She would never forget the look in his eyes from across the marquee when she had said yes to Pieta's proposal only two hours later. That would be with her until the day she died. The regret at all that had been lost would live in her for ever.

Her foot moved of its own accord as she took the step to him and placed her palm on his warm cheek.

He didn't react. Not the flicker of a muscle.

Matteo stared into eyes puffy from crying but that shone at him, almost pleading.

All the words he'd prepared melted away.

He couldn't even remember getting out of his car.

Her trembling hand felt so gentle on his cheek, her warmth penetrating his skin, and all he could do was drink in the face he'd once dreamed of waking up to.

A force too powerful to fight took hold of him, like a fist grabbing his insides and squeezing tightly.

Suddenly he couldn't remember why he hated her. All thoughts had evaporated. All he could see was her, Natasha, the woman he had taken one look at nearly eight years ago and known his life would never be the same again.

CHAPTER TWO

THE WORLD AROUND them blocked itself out and, without a word being said, Matteo crossed the threshold, kicked the door shut behind him and lifted her into his arms.

Their eyes locked together. Her fingers burrowed in the nape of his neck and he carried her up the stairs and into a bedroom. There he laid her on the bed and, his heart hammering in his throat, closed his eyes and brought his lips to hers.

Her taste...

When she parted her lips and his tongue swept into her mouth, the sweet, intoxicating taste he'd never forgotten filled him and from that moment he was lost.

In a frenzy of hands and heady kisses, they stripped each other's clothes off, items thrown without thought, a desperation to be naked and for their bodies to be flush together. Then he speared her hair with his fingers and crushed her mouth to his, teeth and tongues clashing as if they were trying to peel the other's skin and climb inside.

There were no thoughts, no words, only this potent madness that had them both in its grip.

He cupped her small perfect breasts then took them into his mouth, her moan of pleasure soaking right into his bloodstream. He ran his hands over her smooth belly and followed it with his tongue before going lower to inhale her musky heat.

He devoured her, not an inch of her creamy skin with the texture of silk left untouched or without his kiss.

Never had he experienced anything like this, this combustible, primal need to taste her, mark her, to imprint himself into her.

To worship her.

Natasha was adrift in a world she'd never been to before, Matteo her anchor, and she clung to him as if he were all that was left to hold onto, dragging her fingers through his hair, touching every bit of smooth skin she could reach with her needy hands. Every touch seared her, every kiss scorched.

His kiss from seven years ago had flicked something on inside her, a heat that had briefly smouldered before the direction of her life had extinguished it. Now he'd switched it back on and it engulfed her, flames licking every part of her, heat burning deep inside her, an ache so acute she didn't know where the pleasure ended and the pain began. She could cry with the wonder of it all. All those years of living without this…

And it wasn't enough. She needed more. She needed everything.

As if sensing her thoughts, Matteo snaked his tongue back up her stomach and over her breasts, climbing higher to find her mouth and kiss her with such passion that it sucked the air from her lungs.

His hand found her thigh and pushed it out while she moved the other and wrapped her legs around him.

His erection brushed her folds and she gasped

for breath at the weight and hardness of it then gasped again when he pushed his way inside her.

There was no pain, there was too much heat and fire racing through her for that, just a slight discomfort as her body adjusted to this dizzying newness.

And then there was a moment of stillness from Matteo, a pause in the frenzy.

Suddenly terrified he'd sensed or felt something wrong, she grabbed the back of his head and kissed him deeply, hungrily.

And then she forgot to worry, forgot about everything but this moment, this time, and welcomed his lovemaking, the feel of him inside her, the pleasure taking over, taking her higher and higher until the pulsations burst through her and rippled into every part of her being.

As she absorbed these beautiful sensations with wonder, Matteo's movements quickened, his lips found hers and with a long moan into her mouth, he shuddered before collapsing on her.

For a long time they simply lay there, still saying nothing, the only sound their ragged breaths and the beats of their hearts echoing together through their tightly fused bodies.

Then, as the sensations subsided and the heat that had engulfed them cooled, something else took its place.

Horror.

She heard Matteo swallow into her neck, then his weight shifted and he rolled off her, swung his legs over the bed, and swore, first in his native Italian and then in English.

Coldness chilled her skin.

It was just as well she was lying down for if she'd been on her feet she was certain her legs would have given way beneath her.

What had they just *done*?

How had it happened?

She couldn't explain it. She doubted he could either.

Feeling very much that she could be sick, she stared up at the ceiling and tried to get air into her tight lungs. If she could get her vocal cords to unfreeze she might very well swear too.

After a few deep breaths to steady himself,

Matteo got to his feet and went in search of his discarded clothing.

He needed to get out of this house. Right now.

He found his shirt under her dress. One of his socks was rolled in a nest with her bra.

Nausea swirled violently inside him.

What had they just done?

Why the hell had he got out of his damned car? Why hadn't he driven off?

He pulled on his black trousers, not bothering to do the button up, then shrugged his shirt on, not caring it was inside out.

His other sock had rolled half under the small dressing table that had only a thin glass of dried flowers on it. That this was clearly a guest room was the only mercy he could take from this.

Stuffing his socks into his jacket pocket, he slid his feet into his brogues and strode to the door. Just as he was about to make his escape a thought hit him like a hammer to the brain.

His hands clenched into fists as recriminations at his complete and utter stupidity raged through him, every curse he knew hollering in his head.

Slowly he turned around to look at her.

She hadn't moved an inch since he'd rolled off her, her hands gripping the bedsheets, her eyes fixed on the ceiling. But then, as if feeling the weight of his gaze upon her, she turned her face towards him and wide, terrified eyes met his.

That one look confirmed everything.

It didn't need to be said.

Natasha knew as surely as he did that the madness that had taken them had been total.

They had failed to use protection.

And he knew as surely as she did that Natasha wasn't on the Pill. Pieta himself had told him they were trying for a baby.

A thousand emotions punching through him, he left without a single word exchanged between them, strode quickly across the street and into his car.

Only when he was alone in it did the roar of rage that had built in his chest come out and he slammed his fists onto the steering wheel, thumping it with all the force he could muster, then gripped his head in his hands and dug his fingers tightly into his skull.

Another twenty minutes passed before he felt even vaguely calm enough to drive away.

He didn't look at the house again.

Two weeks later

It was taking everything Natasha had not to bite her fingernails. It was taking even more not to open one of the bottles of Prosecco that had been in the fridge since Pieta's funeral. She hadn't drunk any alcohol since the wake. If she started drinking she feared she would never stop.

Francesca was due any minute to go through the plans for the hospital they were going to build in Pieta's memory. To no one's surprise it had taken her sister-in-law only one week to buy the site and get the necessary permissions to develop on it. Her sister-in-law was possibly the most determined person Natasha knew and she wished she had an ounce of her drive and a fraction of her tenacity.

For herself, she seemed to have lost whatever drive she'd ever had. She felt so tired, like she could sleep for a lifetime.

Where this lethargy had come from she didn't

know, had to assume it was one of those stages of grief she'd been told to expect. Everyone was an expert on grief, it seemed. Everyone was watching her, waiting for her to crumble under the weight of it.

And despite everything, she *was* grieving, but not for the reasons everyone thought. Her grief was not for the future she had lost, but the seven years she and Matteo had both wasted.

Mixed in with it all was that awful sick feeling in her belly whenever she remembered how the night of the funeral had ended.

God, she didn't want to think about that but no matter how hard she tried to block the memories, they was always there with her.

The bell rang out.

She blew a long puff of air from her lungs and tried to compose herself while the housekeeper let Francesca in.

Footsteps sounded through the huge ground floor of the house Natasha had shared with Pieta and then Francesca entered the study with her brother, Daniele. It was the figure who appeared behind her brother-in-law that almost shattered the poise Natasha had forced on herself.

As was the custom with her Italian in-laws, exuberant kisses and tight embraces were exchanged with whispered platitudes and words of comfort. Then it was time to greet Matteo.

Bracing herself, she placed a hand loosely on his shoulder, felt his hand rest lightly on her hip as they leaned in together to go through the motions of something neither could forgo without arousing suspicion. When the stubble on his warm jaw scratched her cheek she was hit by the vivid memory of that same cheek scratching her inner thigh and had to squeeze her eyes tightly shut to block the image, something she *must* forget.

But she could smell his skin and the scent of his cologne. Smell him. Feel the strength of his body, the curls of his dark hair between her fingers...

It had been a terrible mistake, something neither of them had needed to vocalise.

She didn't know it was possible for someone to hate themselves as much as she hated herself.

She owed Pieta absolutely nothing, she knew that, but…

She just couldn't believe it had happened. Couldn't believe she had lost all control of herself, couldn't work out how it had happened or why.

It was as if some madness had taken hold of them both.

For one hour she had left behind the girl who had done everything she could to please her parents to the point of abandoning the life she'd so desperately wanted, and had found the hidden woman who had never been allowed to exist.

Protection had been the last thing on either of their minds.

They'd been stupid and so, so reckless.

Francesca hadn't said she would be bringing her brother and cousin with her. It hadn't occurred to Natasha to ask. Daniele and Matteo both ran enormously successful businesses that took them all over the world. She'd assumed their input for the hospital—especially Matteo's—would come at a later date.

But then she looked properly at Francesca and

understood why Daniele at least had stuck around in Pisa. Her sister-in-law looked more bereft than she had at Pieta's funeral. More than bereft. Like the light that had always shone brightly inside her had been extinguished. Daniele would never leave his sister in this state.

And Francesca looked closely at Natasha in turn. 'Are you okay? You look pale.'

She gave a rueful shrug. None of them could pretend they were okay. 'I'm just tired.'

'You're holding your back. Does it hurt?'

'A little.'

The housekeeper brought in a tray of coffee and biscotti, which distracted them all from Natasha's health. They sat around the large dining table onto which Francesca placed a stack of files.

Natasha couldn't even remember what the meeting was for. Matteo being under the same roof as her had turned her brain into a colander.

Why had he come? Was it to punish her?

Every time she'd seen him over the past seven years had been a punishment she'd accepted. She'd let him kiss her and then hours later had agreed to marry someone else, in front of him, in front of everyone. Not just someone else, but his cousin and closest friend. She'd let the moment when she should have told him about Pieta slip by in the haze of his kiss.

Would things have been different if she'd told him, either then or in the weeks beforehand when Pieta's intentions had suddenly become clear? Or would the outcome have been the same?

She'd called and left dozens of messages but Matteo had never answered and he'd never responded. He'd cut her off as effectively as he'd wielded his scalpel.

If things had been different, though, would her life have been any happier? She'd long stopped believing that. Matteo wasn't the man she'd thought him to be. He wasn't a man any woman with an ounce of sanity would consider spending her life with unless she was a masochist. It wasn't just a love of wealth he'd developed since the days she'd fancied herself in love with him; he'd developed a hedonistic streak to match it. No man who had a new woman on his arm every week could ever be content to settle down with only one.

Daniele took control of the meeting, explaining where they were with the project and how he and Matteo were planning a trip to Caballeros in the next couple of weeks. It was hoped construction would begin soon after.

'That quick?' Natasha found the energy to ask.

'It's Caballeros, not Europe,' Daniele answered with a shrug. 'Bureaucracy doesn't exist there in the way we know it.'

'Have you had any publicity ideas?' Francesca asked, reminding Natasha of the role she'd agreed to take in the project.

'I'm sorry, but no.' She stared at the polished surface of the table in her shame. All she'd done these past two weeks was drift. 'I'll get thinking and send you some ideas over the next few days.' She rubbed her temples, hoping she wasn't promising something she would fail to see through. The more publicity they had for it the more donations they would receive, the more donations they received the more staff they could employ.

Dull thuds pounded behind her eyes. As Pieta's next of kin this was her responsibility. Everything concerning her husband's foundation now rested on her shoulders and so far she'd abdicated all responsibility for it.

She would abdicate that responsibility for ever if it was in her power.

At some point soon she would have to think things through clearly but right now her head was so full yet so loose that she could hardly decide what she wanted to eat for her breakfast never mind make decisions that carried real importance.

She couldn't carry on like this. She didn't know if it was shock at Pieta's death or what had happened with Matteo that had her like this but she had to get a grip on herself.

There was a whole new future out there waiting for her and sooner or later she needed to figure out what she wanted from it. So far, all she knew with any real certainty was that she would spend it alone. She would never remarry. She would never allow anyone, not a man, not her parents, to have control over her again.

Francesca raised a weary shoulder. 'There's no rush. The end of the week will be fine.'

Eventually the ordeal was over. Chairs were

scraped back as her family by marriage rose to leave. Following suit, Natasha rose too but as she stood, a wave of dizziness crashed over her and she grabbed hold of the table for support.

Francesca, who'd been sitting next to her, was the first to spot something amiss and took hold of her wrist. 'Are you okay?'

Natasha nodded, although she felt far from okay. 'I'm just tired. I should probably eat something.'

Francesca studied her a while longer before letting her go. 'You know where I am if you need me.'

Considering that Francesca looked as bad as Natasha felt, the suggestion was laughable, but it had come from her sister-in-law's kind heart so she would never laugh at her even if she had the energy.

Burning under Matteo's equally close scrutiny, she found she could only breathe normally when the front door closed behind them.

Needing to be alone, she sent the housekeeper out to do some errands and sent silent thanks to Pieta for agreeing with her request that their other staff not live in. How sad was it that she had to request such things, like a child asking a favour from a parent?

Everything about her marriage had been sad. Its ending was the least of it. She'd had no autonomy over any of it.

Now the dizziness had passed she realised she was famished. She'd felt a little nauseous when she'd woken and had skipped breakfast, which had saved her the worry of deciding what to eat, and had managed to forget to have any lunch.

Opening the fridge, she tried to think what she fancied to eat. The housekeeper had stocked up for her and there was choice. Too much choice. After much dithering she took a fresh block of cheese out, then found the biscuits to go with it.

Her stomach was growling by the time she unwrapped the cellophane from the cheese but when she took the knife to it, the smell it emitted turned the growl into a gurgle that flipped over violently.

She chucked the entire block of cheese into the bin then clutched her stomach with one hand and her mouth with the other, breathing deeply, willing the nausea away.

It had only just passed when the doorbell rang.

She stood frozen, hesitant over whether she should open it. Her house had been like Piccadilly Circus for the past two weeks and all she wanted was to be on her own.

It rang again.

What if it was her mother-in-law? Vanessa had been a frequent visitor since Natasha and Pieta had married, and had visited or called daily since his death. Whatever Natasha was going through was nothing compared to what Vanessa was living with.

And yet, even though she continued to tell herself it was bound to be her adorable mother-in-law at the door, she found she couldn't draw the least bit of surprise to find Matteo there instead.

'What do you want?' she asked, tightening her hold on the door frame. There was no audience for them to pretend cordiality.

'I want you to take this.' He held up a long, thin rectangular box.

It was a pregnancy test.

CHAPTER THREE

THE PALE FACE that had opened the door to Matteo turned whiter. 'I'm not pregnant.'

'Take the test and prove it. I'm not going anywhere until you do.'

Her gaze darted over his shoulder.

'Expecting someone?' he asked curtly. 'Another lover, perhaps?'

Her lips tightened but she held her ground. 'Vanessa likes to drop in.'

'The grieving mother checking up on the grieving widow? How charming.' It sickened him that his aunt—like the rest of the Pellegrinis—all thought the sun rose and set with Natasha. It had been Francesca's worry and compassion towards the young widow that had set the wheels in motion for the events that had led him here today. 'If you don't want her to find me here and have to explain why I have this with me, I suggest you let me in.'

A long exhalation of breath and then she stepped aside.

For the second time that day he entered Pieta's home with the same curdle of self-loathing as when he'd entered it the first time. Revulsion. At her. At himself. At what they'd done.

Until Pieta had died Matteo had been in this house only once, when Natasha had been in England, visiting her parents.

'Have you had a period since…?' He couldn't bring himself to finish the question.

Colour stained her white face at the intimacy of what he'd asked. 'No,' she whispered.

'When are you due?'

Her throat moved before she answered. 'A couple of days ago. But I've never been regular. It doesn't mean anything.'

'You're tired. You have a backache. You used the bathroom three times during our two-hour meeting.' He ticked her symptoms off his fingers dispassionately, although his head was pounding again. They'd made love at her most fertile time. 'My flight back to Miami leaves in three hours. Take the test. If it's negative I can leave Pisa and we can both forget anything happened between us.'

Neither of them said what would happen if the test proved positive.

He held the box out to her. She stared at it blankly for a moment before snatching it out of his hand and leaving the reception room they were still standing in. Her footsteps trod up the stairs, a door shut.

Alone, Matteo took himself to the day room and sat on the sofa, cradling his head in his hands while he waited. In the adjoining room was a bar where he and Pieta had had a drink together. The temptation to help himself to a drink now was strong but not strong enough to overcome his revulsion. He'd already helped himself to his best friend and cousin's wife. He wasn't going to add to his list of crimes by helping himself to Pieta's alcohol.

He'd read the instructions himself. The test took three minutes to produce an answer.

He checked his watch. Natasha had been upstairs for ten minutes.

The seconds ticked past like minutes, the minutes like hours. All he had to occupy his mind were the furnishings the man who'd been like a brother to him had chosen. He couldn't see any sign of Natasha's influence in the decoration.

She'd once wanted to be an interior designer. He remembered her telling him that during a phone conversation held when he'd returned home after an eighteen-hour shift.

Matteo had thought he could never hate himself more than he had when he'd been ten and his dereliction of duty had ruined his little brother's life. The loathing he felt for what he'd done with Natasha matched it, an ugly rancid feeling that lived in his guts. The loathing he felt for Natasha matched it too. Damn her, but she'd been Pieta's wife. Hours after burying her husband she'd thrown herself into his arms and he...

Damn him, he'd let her.

He wished he could erase the memories of that night but every moment was imprinted in him. He'd woken that morning with the vivid feeling of entering her for the first time and the certainty that something had been wrong. It was a feeling that nagged at him more, growing stronger as time passed.

He rubbed the nape of his neck and cursed his fallible memory.

Natasha had been no virgin. She'd been married, for heaven's sake, and had been trying for a baby with her husband.

Another five minutes passed before he heard movement.

She appeared in the doorway.

One look at her face told him the answer.

'There's got to be some mistake,' Natasha croaked, clinging onto the door frame for support. 'I need to do another test.'

She'd stared at the positive sign for so long her eyes had gone as blurry as the cold mist swimming in her head.

For two weeks she'd refused to believe it could happen. She'd refused to even contemplate it.

They had been reckless beyond belief but surely, *surely* nature wouldn't punish them further for it? Surely the guilt and self-loathing they both had to live with was punishment enough?

Eyes of cold green steel stared back at her. It was a long time before he spoke.

'That test is the most accurate one on the market. If it's showing as positive then you are pregnant. So that leaves only one issue to be resolved and that's determining who the father is.'

Afraid she was going to faint, she sank onto the floor and cuddled her knees.

'When did you and Pieta last...?' The distaste that laced his voice as he failed to complete his sentence sent a wave of heat through her cold head.

For the first time in her life she didn't know what to say or do. Whenever life had posed her with a dilemma the answer had always been clear. Do what her parents wanted. It was why she'd married Pieta.

But now her parents were the least of her considerations.

'Do I take your silence to mean that you and Pieta were active until his death?'

How could she answer that? She *couldn't*.

'If your last period was a month ago then it stands to reason you and I were together when you were at your most fertile. However, all women's cycles differ to a certain degree so if you and Pieta were intimate until his death there's a good chance he could be the father. Who else is in line?'

Her head spinning at the medical knowledge that meant he had a much better understanding of how her body worked than she did, she didn't understand what he meant. 'What?'

'Don't pretend you don't know what I mean. Who else have you had sex with in the past month?'

She recoiled. 'That's offensive.'

His laughter crackled between them like a bullet. 'Don't get me wrong, you're playing the grieving widow admirably but you were like a dog on heat with me so it stands to reason there have been others.'

A dog on heat?

She covered her ears, digging her nails into her skull.

A dog on heat?

How had he not *known*? And him a doctor?

There had been a moment, when he'd first entered her, that he'd stilled, but it had only been a moment, and then she had kissed him again, as desperate for him to continue what they'd started as she had been terrified he would figure out the truth.

'I'm waiting for an answer.' His curt voice cut through her thoughts. 'How many others?'

She remembered a time so long ago when his rich voice, the Italian accent faint behind the impeccable English, had always softened around her. She guessed that's what happened when you created a business reputed to be worth billions out of nothing, your basic humanity was thrown in the gutter along with your principles.

'No one.' She raised her head to look him square in the eye. 'There has been no one else.'

He stared back for the longest time before nodding and getting to his feet. 'A scan will pinpoint the date of conception to a degree of accuracy so we can use that to determine who the likely father is.'

His cutting tone sliced through her.

Then the thought of a scan, of seeing the little one growing inside her...

Suddenly it hit her that she was pregnant.

She was going to be a mother.

Placing a hand to her belly, she blurred out Matteo's bitter face and imagined the life growing inside her.

Hello, my little one, she said silently to it, overwhelming joy spreading through every part of her.

She'd wanted a child for so long. After everything that had gone on with Pieta she had thought it would be a long and torturous road to get there if it ever happened and if she'd ever decided to take the road he'd wanted to conceive one. But it had happened as if by magic.

She was going to have a baby.

'How can you be smiling at such a time?' Matteo said acidly. 'Is this amusing to you?'

The smile she hadn't even known she was wearing fell but as it fell her spine straightened.

Whatever the future held for her, even if it was only humiliation, she had her little seed to think about. She couldn't fall into despair. She would be strong. She would be a mother.

'I'm pregnant,' she said, eyeballing him. 'You cannot know how long I have wanted this so, yes, I will smile and rejoice at my child's conception because it is a miracle.'

His jaw clenched, Matteo eyed her back with mirrored loathing. 'You intend to keep it, then?'

Of all the stuff he'd thrown at her, this was by far the cruellest. 'How can you ask such a thing?'

He breached the distance between them and placed a hand round the nape of her neck. Bringing his face close to hers as if examining her, he said with icy quiet, 'Because I know you, Natasha. You're selfish. You think only of yourself and what advances you.'

Stunned into silence at his closeness, at the warmth of his skin on hers, the fingers almost absently stroking her neck, memories of their one time together crashing through her, Natasha had to blink to get her brain back in gear. Breathing heavily, not taking her eyes from his, she raised her arm to find the hand laid so casually on her and dug her nails in as hard as she could as she shoved it away.

Raising herself to her full height, which was almost a foot shorter than his six-feet-plus frame, she said as icily as she could through the tremors in her voice, 'You don't know me at all. If you did you wouldn't have to ask if I wanted to keep it. I will do more than keep it. I will raise it and I will love it.'

Once she had longed for this.

If her eighteen-year-old self had been told that in seven years she would be carrying Matteo's child she would have danced for miles with joy.

But she couldn't tell him that. He wouldn't believe her if she did.

He rubbed the flesh of his hand where she'd stabbed him with her nails.

'I hope for your child's sake that your words aren't as worthless as they usually are but time will tell on that. I've a friend who runs a clinic near mine in Florence with the newest, most accurate scans. I'll take you there. She'll be able to pinpoint the date of conception to at least determine if I'm in the frame as father. Her discretion will be guaranteed and I think one thing we can be in agreement on is the need for discretion.'

Natasha forced herself to breathe.

Everything was happening so quickly. She couldn't let him railroad her but likewise she had to do what was best for her and her baby and until she'd decided what she was going to do, she needed all the discretion she could get.

Oh, God, the implications were too awful to think about.

How many lives were going to be ruined when the truth came out?

The worst of it was she would never be able to tell the full truth. No one could know.

Like Matteo couldn't know that she already knew of an excellent clinic, this one in Paris, where discretion was also guaranteed.

And he couldn't know that he was the only man in the frame for the father of her baby.

Fighting back another bout of dizziness, she nodded sharply. She had to keep it together. 'When?'

'In a fortnight. The baby's heartbeat should be detectable by then.'

'So soon?' She'd known for twenty minutes that she was pregnant and he was saying her baby's heart was already forming? That was just mind-blowing.

He nodded grimly. 'Pregnancy is taken from the date of your last period so in a fortnight you will be classed as six weeks pregnant. Only the scan will be able to give us a reasonably accurate conception date.'

'And I'll be able to hear the heartbeat?'

'We both will.' His face a tight mask, he headed for the door. 'I'll be in touch.'

Only when she heard the door close did she sink onto the sofa and hang her head between her knees.

Soon she would be hanging it in shame.

All the people who were going to be hurt, Vanessa, Francesca... Ever since she'd married Pieta she would catch them looking at her belly, knew they were searching for the signs of swelling, the signs of life growing inside her. Since he'd died the stares had become more obvious. She knew how badly they wished she was carrying Pieta's child. Francesca was already suspicious.

She sat back and rubbed her temples.

She didn't have a clue how to handle this. Whatever she did, everyone would be hurt. Hopes were going to be raised then not just dashed but crushed. Then there was the Pellegrini estate itself...

This was too much.

Overwhelmed by the jumble of thoughts raging through her head, Natasha burst into tears.

It had to be like this, she told herself, hugging her belly, the urge to protect her little seed already strong, even if only from her tears.

The real unvarnished truth would destroy every single one of them, Matteo included.

Better to take it on the chin and have the world, including her own parents, think her a slut than for that to happen. She could hardly bear to think of the disdain and disappointment in their eyes when they learned she was pregnant and that Pieta wasn't the father.

Marrying Pieta was the only thing she'd done in her twenty-five years that had pleased them. It had given them the opportunity to brag to the world that the great Pieta Pellegrini was their son-in-law and it was an opportunity they never let pass by.

Natasha dried her eyes and blew out a long breath.

All the tears in the world wouldn't change things. She was going to be a mother and that meant she had to be strong for her child's sake.

And all the tears in the world didn't change the fact that it was better for the world to think her a slut than for everyone to know that Matteo was the only candidate for father of her baby.

The world could never know that she had been a virgin until the night she'd buried her husband.

The clinic Matteo had booked them into was tucked away in a beautiful medieval building in the heart of Florence. To the unwitting passer-by it could be home to any of the numerous museums and galleries the city was famed for.

The interior was a total contrast. No one entering could doubt they were in a state-of-the-art medical facility.

The cool receptionist made a call and moments

later Julianna, the clinic's director, stepped out of a door to greet them.

Matteo had met Julianna, a tall, rangy woman in her midforties, a number of times at conferences. They welcomed each other like old friends, exchanging kisses along with their greetings.

Then he introduced her to Natasha and they were taken through to the pristine scanning room where everything was set up for them.

'Are you happy for Dr Manaserro to stay in the room while we do this?' Julianna asked Natasha in English.

Her eyes darted to him with an inflection of surprise before she shrugged her slim shoulders. He doubted she'd ever heard him addressed by that title before.

'You will be a little exposed,' Julianna warned.

Another shrug. 'He can stay if he wants,' she answered tonelessly.

Matteo experienced a pang of guilt that was as unwelcome as it was unexpected.

Today was the first time he'd seen Natasha in two weeks. In the intervening period, other than arranging this scan, he'd done his best to forget her and the pregnancy.

The chances of him being the father were extremely slim, he'd reasoned. Even if the scan confirmed that he could be, he still knew it wasn't likely. They'd only been intimate the once whereas Natasha and Pieta must have...

His guts twisted violently as he thought of all the times they must have been together over the years. Pieta and Natasha had been actively trying for a baby. Pieta had told him that the last time he'd seen him.

And she was happy to be pregnant. She'd called it a miracle. Was that because of her longing for a child or because she was happy that a part of Pieta might be living inside her? Surely she must have felt *some* affection for her husband, whatever her actions the night of his funeral?

Surely she wouldn't have reacted like that if she'd thought there was any chance *he* might be the father?

Dio, he shouldn't be thinking like this. It felt too rancid inside him.

Since she'd accepted Pieta's proposal hours

after their one kiss, he'd pushed Natasha out of his mind, never thinking of her, never thinking of her and Pieta together. Only when he'd been in her presence had his loathing of her come out of the compartment in his head he'd put her in, and on those occasions he'd learned to hide it by ignoring her wherever possible. He'd moved on very quickly and in any case Pieta was too good a friend and too close a cousin for Matteo to let a woman come between them.

Pieta hadn't known Matteo and Natasha had been building a long-distance closeness which, looking back, had been strange as he and Pieta had often swapped stories about women. At the time it had felt too...special to be spoken of, which with hindsight had been comical. He must have been caught in a bout of sentimentality and had made sure never to have such ludicrous thoughts again.

If it was indeed Pieta's child then he too would celebrate to know a part of his best friend lived on, even if the mother the child had to live on through was a deceitful bitch.

It *had* to be Pieta's. The alternative…

It would destroy everything.

So he'd left her alone and fought the urge to call every five minutes and make sure she was eating and sleeping properly.

Looking at her now, he didn't think she'd had a square meal since he'd last seen her.

'Okay, Natasha, you are looking at this as a dating scan, I believe?' Julianna said.

She nodded.

'Have you seen a doctor or a midwife yet?'

She shook her head.

'Are you thinking of having the child here or in England?'

Her eyes darted to him again.

Julianna smiled reassuringly. 'It's okay, there are no right or wrong answers.'

'I haven't thought that far ahead,' she whispered.

'You have plenty of time to decide but you should be monitored. The obstetrician we employ here is the best in Florence or I can recommend a female for you if that would suit you better?'

Matteo, feeling perspiration break out on his

back, had to bite his tongue to stop himself from cutting in. Now they were here, the ultrasound screen switched on, he wanted to get this over with.

But that appeared to be the end of the questioning.

'Are you ready to do this?'

'Yes.' It was the most animation he'd heard in Natasha's voice since she'd opened the door to him earlier.

'Lie down and lift your top and lower your skirt to your hips so your stomach is exposed.'

Matteo trained his eyes on the screen.

When Natasha was ready, Julianna tucked tissue around her lowered skirt and took her seat.

Even though he wasn't looking directly at her, he saw Natasha flinch when the cold gel was applied to her stomach.

Julianna then picked up the probe and pressed it over the gel. As she worked, all three of their gazes were fixed on the screen.

'There it is!' she said in delight. 'See, Natasha? There is your baby.'

Natasha craned her neck forward, trying hard to see what was there. 'Where?'

'There.' Julianna put a finger to the screen. 'See?'

Natasha really didn't know what she'd been expecting to see—a fully formed miniature baby this soon into the pregnancy was too wild even for her imagination—but had hoped it would be more than a blob. But then Julianna pressed some keys on the keyboard on her desk and the blob came into sharper focus. It was still a blob but there was something more defined about it that got her already racing heart ready to burst out of her.

'Do you want to hear the heartbeat?'

A moment later the most beautiful sound she'd ever heard echoed through the room.

She didn't dare look at Matteo. If there was anything other than joy on his face it would taint this special moment for ever.

So she continued to look at her little walnut now frozen on the screen and listen to its healthy heart beating while Julianna did whatever she was doing on her computer until her eyes blurred and the beats were no longer distinguishable.

Eventually Julianna pushed her chair back and wiped Natasha's belly clean with another, softer tissue.

'I would say that so far everything is looking good and healthy.'

'So far?'

The older woman smiled. 'I am a medical practitioner. We never talk in absolutes. What I can say with all honesty is that right now your child is developing well and you should be happy with that. As for when it's due…' She gave a date at the end of June.

Natasha closed her eyes. When she had searched the internet and put in the date of conception, every site she had visited had given this same due date within its narrow parameters.

From the way Matteo shifted in his seat, he had done the same maths.

He knew the due date made it impossible for Pieta to be the father. The date of conception was firmly after his death.

He knew the baby was his.

CHAPTER FOUR

NATASHA HAD TO wait until they were back in his car before she had an inkling of what Matteo was thinking.

'This changes everything,' he said after a long period of silence.

'Not really,' she refuted quietly. 'You already knew it could be yours.'

'I know, I was praying that it wasn't,' he spat.

She dug her nails into the palms of her hands. She'd had two weeks to prepare for this moment, researching everything she could about pregnancy whilst hiding any nausea or backache from her steady stream of visitors.

If she hadn't been in such shock at the test coming up positive—who could expect to fall pregnant on their very first time of making love?—she would have been able think much more quickly on her feet and not put Matteo through the turmoil he must have been in over the past fortnight. When he'd asked when she'd last been intimate with Pieta her brain had been too frazzled to think of a straight-up lie. How badly she'd wanted to tell him the truth and spare him all the uncertainty.

The truth would shatter him. The truth would shatter everyone.

It had to be this way. As hard and as painful as it was, it was the lesser of two evils.

If there was a hell she would surely be sent to it for all the lies of omission she'd had to tell and would continue having to tell.

'Do you have any idea of the nightmare you've pulled me into?' he said scathingly, driving them out of the city and into the Tuscan hills.

'The nightmare *I've* pulled you into?' she retorted, raising her voice. 'As far as I recall, you were there too. I accept I behaved badly but you behaved badly too so don't you dare place all the blame on me.'

He changed gear with so much force she thought the gearstick would snap.

His jaw clenched, he drove them on in silence.

As a rule, Natasha loved Tuscany. She loved the glimpses of vineyards and olive groves, the old hidden monasteries that would suddenly spring into view, some old and decrepit, others renovated, beautiful whatever their states. Today the scenery passed her by without notice. Not until they entered a town they hadn't travelled through on their way to Florence did she realise he was taking a different route back.

Her heart sinking, she knew where he was taking her.

Sure enough, soon she caught her first view of Castello Miniato, centrepiece of the Pellegrini estate Pieta had inherited in its entirety when his father had died just weeks after their wedding. The estate he'd married her for.

Matteo pulled the car to a stop outside the fortressed wall surrounding the *castello*.

'What do you see?' he asked her roughly.

'Is this a trick question?'

'No.'

'The *castello*.'

She'd married Pieta in these grounds—thankfully not in the *castello*'s chapel as that would have made their marriage even more of a mockery—with a heart that had felt dead. She'd seen the expectation on her mother's face and the silent nod of encouragement to put her best foot forward. She'd felt the pressure of her father's fingers digging into her upper arm, had thought of the vast amounts of money Pieta had given her parents during their long engagement and had dragged her feet towards him.

Pieta had been waiting under the floral arch. His expression had been neutral. It could have been anyone walking towards him.

She wished she'd had the courage to turn on her heel and run.

The *castello* she'd adored for so long, the castle that had fired her young imagination with thoughts of knights and maidens, had been the main reason Pieta had married her. They'd spent only a handful of nights there but she had grown to detest it, a manifestation of the trapped desperation she'd found herself in.

'Why are we here?'

'To remind you of what you married into. The inheritance of this estate is on hold until there is no longer any possibility you're carrying Pieta's child. But it's more than that—they're all waiting to see if you're carrying a part of *him* in you. They're all hoping for it, Vanessa, Daniele and Francesca, and now you are pregnant but it is medically impossible for it to be his, so I am going to ask you this one more time and I want you to think very carefully before giving me your answer. How many other men did you sleep with in the days before and after you and I slept together?'

Blood heating with loathing and humiliation, Natasha forced herself to meet his baleful glare. 'None.'

'You are sure about that? There was no one three days either side of when we were together? This is important, Natasha.'

'I know very well how important it is and I am telling you there was no one. You're the father.'

A low sigh escaped from him as he bowed his head over the steering wheel.

The hard reality of their situation crystallised in him. For two weeks Matteo had been able to tell himself it was too remote a chance for him to be the father. Natasha's vehement denial of there being anyone else held the ring of truth in it.

'I'm going to want a DNA test done when the child's born,' he muttered, thinking aloud, 'if only for my own peace of mind.'

She laughed derisively.

The anger he'd been holding onto spilled over. 'Do you have any idea of the destruction this is going to cause? This isn't just your life, it's mine too. Vanessa took me in when I was thirteen years old and treated me as if I were her own son rather than her husband's nephew. Daniele and Francesca treated me like a brother. This is going to cost me my family so you can be damned sure I want concrete certainty about the paternity if I'm going to lose everyone I love because of it.'

'Stop this right now,' she said tightly. 'I know how much you love them—I love them too, but you *are* the father and no amount of burying your head in the sand can change that.'

His lungs had closed so tightly he had to force air into them.

His phone vibrated. Taking advantage of the distraction, he pulled it from his jacket pocket.

It was an email from Julianna. Attached was a picture of the scan and a brief message asking him to forward it to Natasha.

He opened the attachment and, staring at the tiny life so small the resolution of the attachment struggled to distinguish it in any great detail, he felt a little of his anger deflate.

All the arguing and recriminations in the world didn't change the one undisputable fact that Natasha was pregnant and...

And he was the father.

Something flickered inside him, a bloom that expanded into his chest, up his throat, seeping into his brain, filling him with an emotion he'd never felt before because the emotion had never existed in him before.

He was going to be a father.

How could he deny it?

He couldn't.

Dio, he was going to be a father.

It was his child growing in her belly, no one else's.

It was time to accept responsibility for this because the other undisputable fact was that their child was innocent and deserved all the protection it could get from both its parents and also because Natasha was right. Burying his head would cause more pain to Vanessa and his cousins in the long term.

'We won't be able to keep this a secret for long,' he said, thinking aloud. 'The pregnancy is going to be noticeable soon. People—Vanessa and the family—will assume it's Pieta's. Their hopes will be raised.'

'They're going to be so hurt.' He heard the catch in her voice. 'They're going to hate me.'

'They're going to hate us both, but we can protect them from the worst of it.'

'How?'

'Come to Miami with me. I'm flying to Caballeros with Daniele tomorrow. We should only be there for a couple of days. When I get back I'll take you home with me. We can say you need a break from everything. In a month or so we can tell them you're pregnant with my child. It'll be easier for them to accept we turned to each other for comfort and that a relationship grew naturally than to accept the truth of the child's conception.'

'You want us to lie?'

'No, I do not want us to lie. I despise dishonesty but what's the alternative? Do you want to return to your parents in England and—'

'No.' Her rebuttal was emphatic.

'Then coming with me is the only answer. If you stay in Pisa, and Vanessa and the others think there is even a chance you are carrying Pieta's…' To build their hopes up only to cut them away would be too cruel. 'We need to show a united front starting from *now.'*

'So you do accept the baby's yours?'

'Yes. I accept it's mine and I will acknowledge it as mine. Come with me and I will protect you both, and we will have a small chance of making the pain of what's to come a little less in the family who have shown both of us nothing but love and acceptance. They have suffered enough.'

She rested her head against the window and closed her eyes. He hated that even looking as if she hadn't slept in a month she was still the most beautiful woman he'd ever laid eyes on.

Eventually she nodded. 'Okay,' she said in her soft, clear English voice. 'I'll come to Miami with you. But only for a while. We can fake a burgeoning relationship, I can get pregnant, and then we can split up.'

'We stay together until it's born.'

Her eyes flew open to stare at him with incredulity. 'That's seven and a half months away.'

'This is your first pregnancy. You need my support.' He remembered his early hospital rotation in the ER when he'd been a junior resident. He'd dealt with numerous pregnant women admitted with complications, knew first-hand that pregnancy was unpredictable.

'Support? You were talking about a DNA test only a few minutes ago. If that's your idea of support, I'd much rather go it alone.'

'Damn it, Natasha, I'd convinced myself there was no way the child could be mine! I wanted it to be Pieta's, I didn't want it to be mine. I wanted to be able to wash my hands of the situation but I can't. I *do* accept it's my baby you're carrying but this isn't going to be easy. Not for either of us. I am not going to let you go through the pregnancy alone, so get that idea out of your head.'

'What happens when it's born?' she demanded to know. 'How much involvement will you want?'

'I don't know!' He thumped the steering wheel in his anger.

This could not be happening. Natasha was having his child. It was going to destroy everything and everyone. But he would not let it destroy his child.

He was going to be a father. He could feel the magnitude of it building inside him.

It had been many years since he'd even considered fatherhood. He'd wanted a wife and a family once, a long time ago when he'd met a woman who'd stolen the breath from his lungs with one look. Until that point he'd been so focused on his surgical career that relationships had passed him by, his affairs with the opposite sex short and on occasion sweet, but never interfering with his focus.

The Rawlings were old friends of his aunt and uncle but the first time he'd personally met them had been during the Christmas period when he'd been in the third year of his residency in a Florida hospital. He'd left Italy at eighteen to study medicine there because it was one of the best medical schools in the world, but had still travelled back to Pisa whenever he could.

He'd arrived late on Christmas Eve, the annual party Vanessa and Fabio threw in their sprawling Pisa villa already well under way. He'd taken one look at the sophisticated, beautiful woman chatting in a group by the enormous Christmas tree and had been instantly enamoured. But then he'd learned that she was only seventeen and had backed right off.

Seventeen? He'd thought she must be at least in her midtwenties.

Being under the same roof meant he'd got to know her a little. What he'd learned had made him want to learn more. Shy on the surface, a little probing had revealed a keen intelligence, a dry sense of humour and a maturity well beyond her years.

He'd returned to America days later, unable to stop thinking about her.

When he'd returned to Italy for Easter, the Rawlings had again been in residence. This time the chemistry between them had been tangible.

He'd left with her phone number and the memory of her making him promise to call as soon as he arrived back in Florida so she wouldn't worry about him arriving safely.

No one had ever worried about him arriving anywhere safely before and it had touched him deeply.

He made the call. It became the first of many. Soon it became a habit to call as soon as his shifts at the hospital were over. They emailed. They wrote. They texted. They lived in different continents but it was only a physical separation. He told her things about himself he'd never shared with anyone. He opened himself up and laid himself bare as he'd never done before.

He was content for them to build a relationship from afar, knowing it wouldn't be long until she came of age and they could be together properly. It was the same for her too, going as far as Natasha looking into universities stateside so they could be together.

Spending over a decade studying and working to achieve his goal of being a surgeon had taught him that nothing worthwhile came easily or could be rushed. To him, Natasha was worth waiting for. It was more than desire, it was a meeting of hearts and minds he could never have explained to anyone because he couldn't explain it to himself. She'd tapped into something in him that he hadn't known existed, a need to create a family of his own. And she'd seen something in him no one else had either. Something good. She knew about the childhood fire that had left his brother so severely disfigured that Roberto had become a recluse, yet had never judged him for his part in it. She'd defended him from himself.

Matteo had always known he would never operate on Roberto himself, even when he qualified as a reconstructive plastic surgeon. Never mind it being unethical, he'd barely coped in the waiting room whenever Roberto had endured the many surgeries and skin grafts he'd needed over the years. To be effective, surgeons needed detachment. He could never have been detached operating on his brother. So he'd researched new techniques and the best surgeons performing them while at the same time researching proven topical remedies for burn scars, determined to come up with something practical that would help his brother. Natasha had had no medical knowledge but had listened and encouraged him.

Discovering that he'd opened his heart and laid himself bare to a lie and that she'd been playing with him had hit him right in the gut. But he'd got over it. He'd hardened his heart against her and had soon considered himself to have had a lucky escape. Since then he'd been far too busy, first finishing his residency and qualifying as a surgeon and then building his businesses, to waste his time thinking about her. Thoughts of a family had been put on the back burner. Life was short and he intended to enjoy it and to hell with the woman who'd played him for a fool.

He didn't deny it had given him satisfaction to imagine her reading the media tales of his self-made wealth and know she would be kicking herself for choosing the wrong cousin.

The irony that she would be the mother of his child after all would be laughable if the situation itself wasn't so tragic.

Taking another long breath, he controlled his tone to say, 'No, I *do* know. I'm going to want full involvement. This is our child and we will raise it together.'

'Together?' Her blue eyes flashed. 'I'm happy for us to raise it as some kind of team but only because I know it's best for the baby, but don't get any ideas about me living with you after it's born or marriage or anything like that because I won't.'

'You have no worries on that score,' he shot back. 'You are the last woman I'd ever consider marrying.'

'Good,' she spat, 'because it will never happen.'

He sucked in a breath, trying to keep a lid on his temper. 'We will work out maintenance and custody arrangements that suit us both and works for our child, but that's a long way off. Right now the priority is for you and I to pretend to be a couple falling in love.'

Her disbelief turned into a bark of bitter laughter. 'You? In love? As if anyone in their right mind would believe that. You're pictured with a different woman every week.'

'I will do whatever is necessary to protect my family and if that means being celibate while we fake a relationship then that's a sacrifice I'm prepared to make. We have to make this convincing.'

His uncle and aunt had taken him in when he'd been at his lowest, when the tension between himself and his father had become a poisonous living being. Fabio and Vanessa had loved him and cared for him as if he'd been a child of their loins. He wouldn't be able to protect Vanessa from the horror of Natasha's pregnancy but he could at least spare her and his cousins the truth of its conception and spare their hopes from flaring that a part of Pieta still lived on through her.

'I'm prepared to make some sacrifices but what about you?' he asked, turning it back on her. 'Can you make people believe the grieving widow is capable of finding love again so soon after burying her beloved husband?'

Instead of displaying the vehement outrage he was sure would come at him, Natasha covered her forehead with her hand. 'Trust me, I am an expert at faking things.'

Natasha sat in the living room waiting for the doorbell to ring. Her bags were packed, her affairs in order, passport at the ready, everything done to uproot her life for the foreseeable future.

Matteo's solution, as much as it troubled her to think of living under his roof, was the best way forward. Really, it was the only way. Francesca's unexpected visit just fifteen minutes after Matteo had dropped her home after the scan had proved that.

Francesca had come to tell her in person that she was getting married. Even with her own troubles and the guilty ache in her heart evoked just by being with her sister-in-law, Natasha had been taken aback by the news. Francesca had had a life plan in which getting married had been relegated to occur at least a decade from now. She hadn't planned on falling in love, though, and although she'd tried to mute her happiness, her radiance shone as brightly as the enormous rock on her wedding finger.

Her understandable self-absorption had stopped Francesca scrutinising Natasha with her usual zeal and she had left without asking if she'd had any publicity ideas yet for the hospital in Caballeros or even checking her out for signs of physical change, for which Natasha had been thankful.

For the first time in her life she'd developed a decent pair of breasts. If these changes were already showing, what would come next? Francesca was training to be a lawyer; inquisitiveness came as naturally to her as breathing. Next time those prying eyes would notice.

Leaving Pisa was the best way forward. She couldn't go home to England. That was unthinkable. She dreaded her parents' reaction when they learned of the pregnancy and the identity of the father as much as she dreaded her in-laws' reactions.

Her parents had forced this marriage on her. They hadn't cared that she'd had feelings for another man, hopes and dreams for a future with him. They hadn't cared when Pieta had dragged their engagement out over six long years. They'd never asked if their marriage was a happy one. If she'd told them the truth about it, they wouldn't have cared. They wouldn't have cared that she'd been trapped with no way out and no means to leave him. There would have been no help from them.

When she'd called her father to inform him of Pieta's death, his first question once the platitudes had been done with was to ask if she could be pregnant. Her mother had asked the same thing at the funeral.

Not even her mother-in-law had been so insensitive to ask that and it was her son who'd died.

Her parents' hopes for a pregnancy had nothing to do with any longing for a grandchild. For them it was all about the money.

So, yes, Matteo's option was the only sensible one.

Sensible and right. Right for her baby.

For all his hostility and for all the fallout he would endure, he wasn't shirking his responsibility. After what had seemed like hopeful beginnings for them, they'd been on the fringes of each other's lives for almost eight years and had spent one incredible night together. They both bitterly regretted that night. They didn't know each other. They didn't trust each other. They needed to use this time to form some kind of relationship that would allow them to raise their child in the spirit of togetherness and not as enemies.

All of this felt rational. Sensible. She needed to put her best foot forward and do her best, as her mother always liked to say, as if she were the leader of some Girl Guide group taking charge on an exciting expedition rather than a mother doing what was best for her child.

Her parents had never done what was best for her; they had always done what was best for them.

She could not live like that any more.

She'd lived her entire life as a pawn to be used, first by her parents and then by her husband, never good enough as she was, never *being* enough as she was, just a sad sap of a girl with a desperation to please.

When her baby was born she would think and do only what was best for it and she would do it on her terms, no one else's. But until then…

Best foot forward and do her best, and don't think about what it would do to her emotionally living with Matteo under his roof. That should be the least of her worries, but when her pulses surged to hear the doorbell ring, she knew it had the potential to be the greatest of all the dangers.

CHAPTER FIVE

MATTEO'S JET, WITH *Manaserro* emblazoned in bold red lettering on its sides, was ready for boarding as soon as they'd been whisked through security. Take-off occurred within minutes.

After showing Natasha all the facilities, including the bedroom, which he said was for her use during the long flight, Matteo settled himself at his desk and turned his tablet on.

He raised his brows when she took the seat opposite. 'Don't you want to get some rest? You look tired.'

That she could not deny. The pregnancy hormones were making her exhausted but she'd been so wound up over the guilt of their plans and all the other things weighing on her conscience that she couldn't switch her brain off to sleep.

'Maybe later. Tell me how it went in Caballeros.'

He shrugged and put his tablet down. 'I can

honestly say I've never been to such a dire country in my life.'

'That bad, was it?'

'Worse. Francesca's fiancé—' He suddenly interrupted himself. 'Did I tell you she spent one week there and fell for her bodyguard? They're getting married.'

Natasha nodded. 'Francesca told me.'

'Her fiancé is not a man to be messed with and the hospital site itself is secure. He's got men permanently posted there for the duration of the construction process but the Caballeron government is corruption itself.'

That came as no surprise. Caballeros was infamous. Ranked the sixth most dangerous country in the world, drugs and crime were rife. Daniele had insisted Francesca, who'd been hell-bent on getting the hospital site approved as a memorial to Pieta, only travel there with heavy protection.

Thinking of Daniele made Natasha chew her bottom lip, the weight of her conscience pressing down extra hard.

'Did you tell Daniele about us?' she asked in a small voice.

He grimaced again and sighed heavily. 'I set the seed and told him you were going to fly out to Miami for a break. He didn't seem to be bothered by it.' Suddenly he slammed his fist down on the desk, real anger on his face. 'How do you do it?' he demanded.

'Do what?'

'*Lie*. Daniele trusts me. It didn't occur to him that I was feeding him a steaming pile of manure. How does it come so naturally to you?'

'It doesn't,' she said, stung. 'I *hate* lying. It's deceitful.'

'Stop the pretence. Lying comes as naturally to you as breathing—you told me yourself that you're a pro at faking things.'

She clenched her teeth together knowing she deserved that comeback. She *had* told him that. He couldn't know she'd been referring to her marriage and the mountain of lies it had been built on.

'It was your idea for us to play it like this,' she reminded him icily, 'and you can't tell me you haven't told a bagful of lies in your time.'

'Not in my personal life.'

'You lie in your professional life?'

'There isn't a physician alive who hasn't told a white lie.'

'And what do your lies consist of? *Yes, your nose is huge, let me shrink it for you and charge you a vast amount for it*?' she taunted. 'Although from what I've heard you're too busy swanning around the world building your empire to bother with the nitty-gritty of surgery itself.'

His green eyes turned icy cold. 'I don't swan around, whatever that means. I employ the best surgeons from the top medical schools in my clinics and we operate under a strict code of ethics. A doctor's first duty is to do no harm and I am insulted you would imply otherwise. I have never lied to a patient but in my residency days I did on occasion lie to a relative at the patient's request, like with the mother who wanted to spare her child from knowing the prognosis of the cancer eating at her brain until she thought the child was in the right place to handle it. Those lies were told to prevent further suffering.'

She stared at his tight, angry face. For the first time in seven years she saw a glimpse of the man he'd been before, the man who'd been passionate and driven about his work, a man she'd thought no longer existed.

'Why did you turn your back on it?' she asked, unable to hide her bewilderment.

'I didn't. I became an entrepreneur alongside it.'

'You were going to be a reconstructive surgeon. You took the most direct routes to it that you could find...'

'And I *am* a reconstructive surgeon. I perform enough to keep my skills sharp, but the surgeons in my employ fix people who are unhappy with how they look. That's what I always set out to do.'

'No, you didn't. You wanted to fix people who were maimed and disfigured. You never said anything about opening your own clinics. The skin cream you wanted to develop was to help your brother...'

'My brother died,' he said, drumming his fingers on the desk, the glint of danger in his eyes.

'I know and I'm sorry.' She knew that when Matteo was ten and his brother Roberto eight, Roberto had been seriously injured in a fire that had left him with horrific internal and external scarring. It was a miracle he'd survived to live another twenty years. When she'd heard of his death she'd known Matteo would be devastated.

Poor Matteo. One minute he must have been on top of the world, qualifying as a surgeon after so many years of hard work, then only three months later, when he'd hardly had the time to taste his success, the brother he'd adored and had longed to make better had died.

She had wanted so badly to reach out to him but had known her words of condolence would not be wanted. They wouldn't be wanted now either.

Adopting a softer tone, she said, 'I just remember all the conversations we used to have. I remember the ideals you had back then.'

'Those?' he mocked. 'They were a young doctor trying to impress a beautiful woman with his humanity.'

Heat spread low inside her at the backhanded compliment. 'So you *are* a liar, then.'

His sensual lips pulled into a smile but the eyes didn't change, holding hers with that dangerous yet somehow seductive glint. 'Not lies. I merely chose to alter the path I was taking. That's the beauty of life—it's full of options, something I am sure you're familiar with. After all, you chose to marry Pieta, heir to the Pellegrini estate, rich in his own right, when there would have been other options available to you. And now you're a reasonably rich widow you will have a pool of men to choose from to make husband number two.' The smile became cruel. 'Or have you already got a man in mind, *bella*? A rich surgeon perhaps who can comfortably keep you in the lifestyle you've become accustomed to?'

Even his endearment of *bella* sounded like a mockery.

'I've already said I don't want to marry you,' she snapped. 'I don't want to marry anyone.'

'But, *bella*, I don't trust a word you say so why should I believe that? If you're secretly hoping my invitation to live with me during the pregnancy means I have some latent feelings for you, you're wrong. I admit that once I did have feelings but you killed them when you accepted Pieta's proposal and I realised you'd been toying with both of us. If I ever marry I would need to trust my wife. I would require some form of loyalty and faithfulness and we both know you're incapable of any of that.'

Natasha's stomach shredded under the weight of his malevolence but she refused to cower under it. 'You haven't lived my life; you know nothing about me. And how dare you speak of loyalty as if it's an attribute you own when you bedded your best friend's wife on the day of his funeral.'

The mocking glint disappeared. Matteo rose to his feet, towering over her, his face dark and menacing. 'That is something I will regret for the rest of my life. You're a gold-digger. You chose Pieta over me because he had money and back then I had little—you see, *bella*, I do know you. I know you come from a greedy, grasping family who spent my cousin's money as if it was going out of fashion and his death means the gravy train is over. You only inherit his personal wealth, substantial, I admit, but nothing compared to the income you enjoyed from the Pellegrini estate when he was alive. Was that why I came back in your favour now I'm so much more than an overworked doctor?'

Matteo watched the colour drain from her face as he spoke but felt no guilt. He only spoke the truth. Pieta had mentioned a number of times about helping Natasha's parents out. He'd described them as leeches.

'You came to *me*,' she hissed, rising too and leaning on the desk between them, blue eyes spitting brimstone. 'You're entitled to your opinions of me—I can't change them, I know that—but you're not entitled to your own facts. You turned up at *my* door, not the other way round. We were both there, we both know what happened just... happened. It wasn't planned and I will not have you twist things round so that you can absolve yourself of any blame. Our child's conception is on both of us so you can damn well stop putting it all on me.'

Matteo threw his head back and clenched his jaw before looking at her.

Dio, even in anger she was beautiful. All she wore was a pair of slim fitting jeans and a navy top that fell off the shoulder, and she still filled his loins with an inexplicable craving.

He wished he had the power to eradicate their night together from his memories.

It hadn't even been a whole night. Barely an hour.

The most explosive, fulfilling hour of his life.

It had been an eruption of desire so intense and all-consuming it should have burnt itself out there and then, not remain simmering in his blood.

Natasha had the potential to drive him out of his mind. She was a Pandora from mythology, beautiful, beguiling, radiating innocence but inside full of deceit. Natasha had the jar in her hand that when opened was going to unleash hell on his earth.

But she was right that it wasn't fair for him to put all the blame on her.

Wasn't that exactly what his father had been doing for twenty-five years, blaming Matteo for the fire rather than accepting his own responsibility for it?

He would never be like his father.

He *had* gone to her. It had been he who'd kept his finger on the buzzer until she'd opened the door. Even now, with a month's distance from the event, he had no insight into his own motives. He still couldn't understand what had compelled him to get out of the car and cross the street to the house.

Whatever the underlying reason, it didn't change the outcome. They were having a baby together.

'You're right,' he said, sitting back down with a sigh. 'The guilt belongs to us both. I shouldn't put it all on you.'

Her stony glare didn't drop an inch.

He rubbed his forehead, trying to ease the pressure building in it. 'Look, the next seven, eight months are not going to be easy for either of us.'

'No, they're not,' she agreed, her voice a fraction calmer.

'Like it or not, our baby ties us together. I've seen first-hand how destructive warring parents can be. I saw it all the time during my residency, parents who could hardly stand to be in the same room as the other even when their child was seriously ill. I don't want our child to suffer because of us. For our baby's sake, I'm willing to try and look past what went on between us before and build some kind of relationship that isn't based on loathing.'

Her eyes flickered. 'Really? You can stop throwing the past back in my face?'

'I can try. I'm never going to trust you but for better or worse we're now always going to be involved in each other's lives. I'm prepared to try. What about you? Are you willing to try too?'

Her gaze didn't leave his but there was a discernible softening in her eyes, a slight crease forming in her brow as if she was thinking.

She stayed like that for a long time.

Then her lips pulled together and her throat moved before she nodded and whispered, 'Yes. I'm willing to try.'

He almost put out his hand to invite her to shake on their truce but stopped himself before his fingers had moved more than a fraction towards her.

It wasn't just his fingers that yearned towards her. It was all of him.

He cleared his throat. 'So now that's settled, would you like me to order you some food?'

She shook her head and looked away. All the

fire that had spilled out of her just a short while ago had been dampened. Now she looked lost.

'I'm not hungry. I think I'll take you up on your earlier suggestion and get some rest.'

'Whatever you wish.'

She walked to his bedroom with a gait that was almost a shuffle. When she reached the door she looked at him again. Even with the distance now between them he could see the crease still in her brow and something that looked like pain in her eyes.

'I know you won't believe me but I never meant for any of it to happen. I never meant to hurt you. I...' She swallowed and bit into her lip.

Something reached out from his chest and clenched around his throat. Suddenly feeling that he could choke, he waved a dismissive hand. 'You didn't hurt me.'

Natasha closed the door behind her and put one clammy palm to her chest, the other to her mouth and blinked back the hot tears that had filled her eyes.

Despite his denial she knew she'd hurt him all those years ago.

She'd hurt them both.

Drained, her head pounding, she pulled the shades down, removed her shoes and lay on Matteo's king-size bed.

Soon these erratic feelings swirling inside her would subside and she'd be able to breathe.

The soft sheets had a delicious freshly laundered scent to them she found comforting.

Matteo had slept in this bed before. Many times.

How many women had slept in it with him?

She squeezed her eyes shut.

She couldn't afford to allow herself to care. Matteo was the father of her child but he could never be anything more. That ship had sailed. Even if it hadn't, and even if she wasn't determined to grab her freedom and live her life free from anybody else's chains, Matteo would not be the one.

If she'd thought marriage to Pieta had been hard she could only imagine the hell Matteo would have put her through.

He thought a few months of celibacy was a *sacrifice*. God alone knew how many times he would have cheated on her if she'd married him. He went through women like most people went through their laundry.

He wasn't the man she'd believed him to be all those years ago. She'd thought him a man of integrity. She'd believed him when he'd said he wanted to be the world's foremost reconstructive surgeon. The life he'd chosen, however, was the antithesis of those early dreams.

No, he most definitely was not the man she'd believed him to be. And now she was fated to be tied to him for the rest of her life.

The first two weeks in Miami passed a lot more easily than Natasha expected. That she was given Matteo's guesthouse at the back of his waterfront home helped. She'd expected to be physically living under the same roof as him but instead had her own place complete with her own private swimming pool. She'd yet to venture any further into his home than the utility and kitchen. They rarely saw each other but when they did they were at great pains to be polite to each other.

So far, their *entente cordiale* was holding up.

Matteo worked long hours. His headquarters and the clinic he personally practised from were only a mile from his home on Biscayne Bay but he made frequent trips across America to his other clinics.

The only real time they had spent together had been a visit to an obstetrician friend of his, who had asked her a myriad of questions and examined her with such a gentle touch that she'd found herself reassured. Whether she had her baby here or in Pisa, she would be in excellent hands.

Pisa…

At some point in the near future they would return there. The plan was for Matteo to return to Caballeros with Daniele when the structure of the hospital was complete. They'd decided that would be the best time to confess the pregnancy.

She was thinking all this as she sat with her legs in the guesthouse pool, soaking up the last of the day's sun, soul music playing gently through the earphones, sipping on fresh orange juice brought to her unasked by a member of his friendly staff. So lost in her own world was she that she didn't hear any sign of another's presence until a shadow crossed over her.

Turning her head, she found Matteo standing over her.

She whipped the earphones out, sloshing juice over her hand in the process.

'Sorry if I frightened you,' he said wryly.

'I wasn't expecting you back yet.'

'I finished sooner than expected.' He'd gone to Los Angeles the day before, preparing to open a new store that would sell his magic creams; the two he already had there were bursting at the seams with clients desperate to hand their money over for the miracle of reducing their crow's feet.

She could still hardly believe that the topical lotion he'd been intent on developing all those years ago to reduce his brother's burn scars had turned into such a phenomenon.

Two years after she'd become engaged to Pieta, Matteo had finally qualified as a surgeon. At some point in those two years he'd found the successful formula because he'd launched the lotion as a skin moisturiser six months after qualifying, only months after Roberto's death. It hadn't just helped reduce burn scars but acne scars and wrinkles too. It had been a word-of-mouth sensation that had gone viral on social media within days. Initially selling online, he'd since cannily resisted the pleas from department stores worldwide to stock it, instead selling it from the medical clinics he'd opened at an alarmingly fast rate and then opening his own dedicated stores.

While she admired the drive and dedication it must have taken to make such a success of himself in such a relatively short time, she'd never forgotten the humble doctor he'd been who'd wanted only to help his brother and be the best surgeon he could be. In all their long talks he'd never once said anything about money being a motivating factor in his life's choices. Of all the choices he'd made since his brother's death—and it was obvious to her that Roberto's death had been the trigger behind the new life Matteo had pursued—this was the one she found the saddest.

From his jacket pocket he produced a paper napkin from a well-known coffee shop chain. Crouching at her side, he took the hand covered with spilt juice and wiped it.

Taken aback at the gesture, Natasha didn't have time to resist.

Her cheeks flaming, both at his unexpected touch and the realisation she was sitting before him in nothing but a one-piece swimsuit, she muttered, 'Thank you.'

'How have you been?' he asked, removing his shoes and rolling his trousers up to sit next to her, dipping his large feet in the warm water.

'Good, thanks.'

'No more dizzy spells?'

'None.'

He nodded. 'Sleeping okay?'

'Yes.' Surprisingly well.

'That's good. You will let me know if you have any concerns or worries?'

'I've already promised that at least ten times.' This had been something else she hadn't anticipated, that Matteo would take such an active interest in the pregnancy. Although they had seen little of each other, he messaged her frequently to check that she was feeling all right and had his staff check on her regularly. The guesthouse was connected to the main house by an enclosed glass walkway and there were intercoms in every room that connected straight to his head of housekeeping, who lived in the staff house. Natasha had her privacy but in her time here she'd never felt lonely or abandoned. And that was something else that surprised her. In Pisa, she'd hated living with staff. She didn't find it at all intrusive coming from Matteo's staff, who were a lot more relaxed and upbeat than those Pieta had employed.

'I'm just reinforcing the message.'

'Consider it reinforced.'

Their eyes met, a brief moment of humour flickering between them before she turned her face away to stare at their feet in the water. She never doubted his concern was all for the health of their growing baby.

'The foundations for the hospital have been completed,' he said.

'Already? That was quick.'

'Bureaucracy doesn't exist in Caballeros. The San Pedro Governor is behind the project so it's all systems go. Daniele's been out there again. He's paying his staff triple time to work through the night.' Natasha remembered the agreement that had been made that Pieta's foundation would pay for the site and that Daniele would pay the construction costs and for his own staff to build it. It would be costing him a fortune.

'You've spoken to him?'

'A number of times. He expects the shell of the building to be done within a month. He wants me to go back with him then, before they start the finishing process and it's too late to make any changes I think are needed from a medical standpoint.'

Matteo leaned back on his arms and breathed in the air, trying to unknot the tension that had become a permanent thing in him and always tightened whenever they spoke of Daniele or the other members of his family.

'Has anything been said? About us?' she asked quietly.

'He asked how you were doing. Said Vanessa was missing you.'

She bowed her head and hunched her shoulders.

'She keeps messaging me,' she whispered then swallowed. A tear rolled down her cheek. She wiped it away with the back of her hand. 'I don't know how to respond. It's the same with Francesca. She's called me three times. I try and keep things light and non-specific but I feel so guilty. They've been so good to me and it's killing me to know I'm going to break their hearts.'

He dug his fingers into the grass, resisting the compulsion to put an arm around her. Natasha evoked feelings in him he couldn't begin to understand. She always had.

He had no control over his body's responses to her; even now he was having to fight his own head to tune out that she was wearing nothing but a pretty striped swimsuit and that before she'd hunched herself over he'd seen a glimpse of breasts that had swollen since he'd last seen her only three days before.

It was the need to resist temptation that had seen him travelling more than normal these past few weeks and working the hundred-hour weeks he'd not done since his residency days. Being with her was too much, a constant battle that veered between wanting to shout and shake her, and wanting to pull her close and make love to her again.

He'd promised to try and put the past behind them but, damn it, it was hard.

But he had made that promise and he knew that however hard it was for him, she would be suffering more. She was carrying their child.

Keeping a distance between them might be good for his state of mind but she was under a huge amount of stress. It might suit him better to cast her as an unfeeling cow but that was far from the truth. His clinics in Los Angeles had seen him cross paths with many actresses, good and bad. He could spot a phoney a mile off. Natasha's distress about the Pellegrinis' reaction to the pregnancy was genuine. He'd brought her to Miami in part to support her through this pregnancy. It was time he started holding up his side of their bargain.

'When was the last time you left this place?'

Startled blue eyes found his. 'What do you mean?'

'According to my staff you rarely go out.'

She managed a weak smile. 'Have you got them spying on me?'

'Not spying, more keeping an eye on you.

You've got too much thinking time on your hands and it's making you worry about something neither of us has any control over. You need to keep busy, *bella*. We can start by going out for dinner. Have you any favourite foods you like?' As he asked the question he remembered a long ago conversation about her love for spicy food. He blinked the memory he hadn't thought of in nearly eight years away.

'I'll eat anything.'

He pulled his feet out of the water and stood up. 'I'll have a think about a decent restaurant. Come over to the main house when you're ready.'

Then he picked up his shoes and walked barefoot into his home.

CHAPTER SIX

NERVES CHEWED NATASHA'S stomach as she walked up the marble steps and into Matteo's vast house. It was the first time she'd gone further than the room she knew was used as a utility but which looked like an art gallery, and one of the kitchens, which had the same feel to it. If one didn't know its purpose you could assume it was anything. The first time she'd gone in it the chef had casually mentioned it was the smallest of the kitchens. Turned out Matteo had three of them.

A member of staff appeared and with a smile took her through the house. As they walked, she gazed around in astonishment at the uniqueness and beauty of it all. The exterior was a work of sleek art in itself, with masses of glass and white stucco, but the interior... Everything flowed, the many staircases gave the illusion of floating...

it was incredible, a work of art come to life. No wonder Daniele, the architectural brain behind it, had won awards for it. At the time of completion, a year ago, it had been valued as the most expensive property in the whole of Miami.

She was taken through to a vast room, the ceiling at least two storeys high and with an abundance of cream sofas and armchairs, easily enough to seat two dozen people with space to spare.

Left to her own devices, Natasha looked out at the spectacular view of the bay, the sky shades of pink under the setting sun. The room seemed to jut out and touch the bay itself.

She turned round and stared up at what appeared to be a floating balcony but which she quickly understood was a walkway that was part of the second floor. What new delights were there to discover up there?

A glass wall that reached all the way up to this strange yet beautiful indoor balcony soon revealed itself to be a cabinet but it was the huge canvas print beside it that really caught her attention and she walked over to examine it in more detail.

The print was a photograph of two beaming young boys, the elder no more than ten, the smaller one only a couple of years younger. They were sitting on a bench, arms wrapped around each other, their cheeks pressed together, identical curly black hair almost fused into one mass.

'Sorry to keep you waiting.' Matteo's rich tones vibrated through the room.

Natasha looked around but couldn't see him.

'Up here.'

Craning her neck, she found him peering down at her from the floating balcony. A wry smile of amusement on his face, he walked the length of the balcony then disappeared from view, reappearing moments later on the other side of the room.

He must have travelled down a staircase hidden from view.

He'd changed into a pair of crisp navy trousers and a light grey open-necked shirt, his tall elegant frame carrying it off with a panache that made her think of Christmas perfume adverts that always featured suave, gorgeous men and lithe beautiful women. It was the swirls of exposed hair coming through the shirt that had her heart pounding so hard. She remembered so vividly running her fingers through that hair...

Swallowing hard as he strode towards her, she turned her attention back to the print and pointed a trembling finger at the older child. 'Is that you?'

He stood beside her and looked at it.

Fresh cologne filled her senses.

'Yes. I was nine when that was taken.'

'And is the other boy your brother?' It was a silly question really as other than the size difference they could have passed for twins.

'Yes.'

There was a long stretch of silence between them.

'I really was very sorry to hear Roberto died,' she said quietly. 'I know how much you loved him.'

They'd briefly mentioned Roberto's death on Matteo's jet over, but the conversation had turned into a spew of bitterness from him that had stopped her saying anything more about it.

If Matteo had been nine in this picture, then the fire that had torn their lives apart must have happened within a year of it being taken.

She blinked back hot tears as she looked at the happy faces of a life gone by.

Many stories had swirled in the aftermath of Roberto's funeral, gossip and whispers between the family members about a spectacular row between Matteo and his father. Natasha knew the two men's relationship had been strained since the fire, knew Matteo thought his father blamed him for the fire, something that had always made her heart wrench and her blood boil.

She'd never learned what the row at the funeral had been about but it had been serious enough for Matteo to legally change his surname within weeks. It could only have been intended as a snub to his parents—Manaserro was Vanessa Pellegrini's maiden name. He'd chosen the family name of his uncle's wife. As far as she was aware, Matteo and his parents hadn't spoken since.

As Matteo stood looking at the last happy picture ever taken of his brother, he knew Natasha was thinking of the fire. He'd told her about it himself during one of their many marathon phone calls. He'd told her everything, how he'd been only ten years old when his parents had gone out for lunch leaving him in charge of eight-year-old Roberto, how Roberto had stolen a box of matches from the kitchen and taken them to the barn at the back of their house without Matteo even noticing he'd left the house, and how Roberto had lit those matches one by one, seeing how long he could keep each flame going. It had been a hot day after a period of hot weeks without any rain. The barn had been a tinder box and Roberto had been lucky to escape with his life.

Matteo had escaped with nothing more than the nightmares of his brother's screams, which had sounded as if they'd been dredged from the bowels of hell itself, and his own screams when he'd heard his brother's and had raced out of the house to find him. The image of his brother's small body engulfed in flames haunted him. If the gardener hadn't acted so quickly to douse the flames, Roberto would have died right before his eyes.

Natasha was the only person he'd shared this

with. He'd never even told Pieta the sheer horror of what Roberto had been through and what he'd seen.

He hadn't held anything back from her, not his father's complete withdrawal of affection towards him, his belief that his parents blamed him for the fire, the increasing arguments and cold hostility that had culminated in him leaving the family home at thirteen to live with his uncle's family, not the visits back home to see his brother that had only been undertaken when his father had been out, not the many surgical procedures Roberto had endured throughout the rest of his life and for which Matteo had always sat in a separate waiting room from his parents.

He'd trusted her. He'd trusted her with everything.

The worst of it was she'd consoled him. He'd thought she believed in him. Her soft voice had given him comfort.

Then she'd taken his trust and ripped it to shreds.

They stood before the picture for a few more moments in silence before Matteo sighed deeply.

It had all happened such a long time ago but sometimes, like now, it might have happened only yesterday.

'Come on,' he said. 'Let's go and eat.'

He led her out to the secure docking bay at the side of his mansion where a gleaming yacht awaited them.

'Is this yours?' she asked with an inflection of surprise.

He nodded and waved a hand to greet the captain awaiting them on deck.

'I've never noticed it before.'

'Have you been round this side of the house?' he said drily.

'No,' she admitted.

'There's your answer.'

'Where are we going?'

He pointed to the island floating in the bay some distance before them. 'Key Biscayne. It's quicker and more pleasurable to sail there rather than drive. How are your sea legs?'

'I guess we're about to find out.'

Within minutes they were standing at the front of the yacht, leaning over the railing as they cut through the water, her blonde hair whipping behind her.

'You like it?' he asked.

She nodded, a wide grin forming, the first real flare of joy he'd seen on her beautiful face in such a long time that it pierced his chest to see it now.

He turned his gaze from her to look at the approaching Key Biscayne. 'Why haven't you explored any of Miami since you've been here?'

'I don't know my way around.'

'I told you when we got here that you only had to ask and a member of staff would be happy to drive you or accompany you anywhere you wanted to go. You're not my prisoner, *bella.*'

'I know I'm not.'

'Then why stay in all the time? Miami is one of the most vibrant cities in the world.'

She shrugged and put a hand to her face to shield herself from locks of thick hair falling into it. 'Where would I go?'

'I don't know. The beach? A café? One of the museums? Jungle Island? An art gallery? A nightclub—there's plenty of those.'

She gave a wry smile. 'I can just see pregnant old me dancing the night away in a sweaty night-club.'

So could he. Vividly. That long honey-blonde hair swaying, that lithe body in the slim-fitting off-the-shoulder blue-and-white-striped dress she was wearing, moving to the music, wrapped around his...

He blinked the image away and took a breath to drive away the burst of heat in his loins.

'You're pregnant, not dead. There's plenty of exclusive clubs here you can go to that aren't the sweaty places you're thinking of.'

'On my own?'

'I'm not speaking literally. I'm just saying you should be making the most of being fit and able to do things while you can. In a few months you'll be waddling like a duck with a watermelon for a belly.'

'You make it sound so delightful. I look forward to waddling like a duck.'

He grinned at her dryness. He didn't think for a minute that Natasha would ever waddle. She had too much elegance.

It struck him then that he would be there to see the changes in her. He would watch her belly ripen and her breasts grow.

He would be there for all of it. Nothing on this earth would make him miss any of it.

He wondered what changes had already happened that weren't yet visible to his eye, what physical shifts Natasha could feel within her.

'Do you really want to spend the pregnancy stuck in my little patch of the earth?' he said in a teasing tone that belied the depth of his thoughts and the emotions shooting through him.

'It's hardly little.'

'You know what I mean.'

She sighed. 'Yes, I do know. There's lots of reasons but the main one is because I'm trying to save money.'

'You're short of cash?'

'If I spend it frivolously I will be. I have no job. I'm pregnant with no employment history so there's no realistic prospect of me getting one in the foreseeable future.'

'I know you won't inherit the *castello* and the

rest of the family estate but you're going to inherit Pieta's personal wealth.'

'I don't want it. It wouldn't be right.'

'Don't be ridiculous. You were his wife. It's yours by right.'

'I could accept that if I'd contributed to it in any way but I didn't. Everything he earned was his and it was all earned without any help from me.'

'You provided a home for him.'

She shook her head, her hair swishing gently around her shoulders. 'The house was his. The staff were his. The furnishings were his and to his taste. Everything was *his*.'

There was an undertone to her words that raised his antennae.

'You were together for seven years,' he said slowly, trying to figure out what that undertone could mean or why something in his gut told him to listen to it.

'But only married for one. We didn't live together until we married. I cannot in all good conscience take that money, especially not now that

I'm having your baby. I could never live with myself.'

His incredulity deepened.

She'd married Pieta for his money. And now she was planning to walk away from it?

A dozen more questions formed but they'd arrived at the dock by the quayside restaurant he'd booked them into so had to wait until they were at their table before he could ask them and the next dozen that formed in quick succession.

They were shown to a table overlooking the waterfront, the distant Miami skyline lighting up like a silhouette under the rapidly darkening night sky.

'This place is so *glamorous*,' Natasha said when they were seated, her eyes too busy darting around the eclectic restaurant to bother looking at the menu she'd been given. 'Have you eaten here before?'

'I brought my Miami staff here for our Christmas party.'

'Lucky staff. The last time I ate out was at a stuffy ambassador's residence.'

'Not glamorous?'

'If you like old-fashioned glamour.'

'You don't?' He thought of her house in Pisa. Pieta had been a collector of antiques, his tastes shining through every item on display. Now he thought about it properly, there had been nothing of the Natasha he had known all those years ago in that house. It was as if her personality had been subsumed by her husband's.

She hesitated before answering. 'Not particularly. I'm more of a modern girl. What do you recommend to eat?'

'The lobster's good.'

She pulled a face. 'Lobster's boring.'

'Really?'

'Too sweet.' She peered at the menu and pulled another face. 'What the heck are Peruvian potatoes?'

'Potatoes from Peru?' he suggested drily.

She met his eye and sniggered. 'Maybe they come wrapped in a llama.'

He grinned. 'You should try them.'

'I will. Seed-crusted halibut, Peruvian potatoes, wild mushrooms, sea beans and red pepper coulis. Perfect.'

Their food ordered, drinks set before them, Matteo settled back and watched Natasha continue her unabashed admiring of the restaurant's decor.

'You know what I don't understand?' he said.

'What?'

'Why you gave up your plans to be an interior designer.'

The amusement that had flared between them faded, to be replaced by wariness. 'It just never happened.'

'Why not? You still did the degree you wanted in it, didn't you?'

He could tell by the look in her eyes she was remembering how seriously she'd been considering moving to America to do her degree at the Art Institute of Tampa. She'd sent him the prospectus. He'd looked at places to live that were commutable for them both.

She gave a slight nod. 'I ended up doing a BA in Interior Architecture and Design.'

'In England?'

Matteo had tried never to discuss Natasha with anyone over the years and he'd limited his trips back to Europe as much as he could, but it had been impossible not to hear chatter about her. By accepting Pieta's proposal she'd been embraced into the bosom of the Pellegrini family. It had been natural for them to pass on information about Pieta's fiancée to him. They'd assumed he would be as interested as they were. Everyone had assumed that once she'd graduated, they would marry. It had taken another three years for that to happen, although Pieta had bought an apartment for her in Pisa, close to his sister's apartment.

Tales of her had rarely come from Pieta himself. If he ever had spoken of her it had usually been in practical terms, never romantic.

She nodded again.

'Why didn't you take it any further once you graduated? Didn't you enjoy it?'

She gave a wistful smile. 'I loved it. I like to think I was good at it.'

'So what stopped you pursuing a career? You were engaged to a well-known man with contacts all over the world. It would have been easy for you to build a client list.'

'I know.'

'So what stopped you?' he repeated. 'Was it just that you preferred being a lady of leisure?'

Something flickered in her eyes before they flitted away from his gaze.

'I'm not picking a fight here, I'm just trying to understand.' He tried to keep his voice reasonable but as he asked the question he could feel the old anger swelling inside.

This was an extension of their earlier conversation and Natasha's insistence that she wouldn't accept her rightful inheritance. She'd spoken with such sincerity that he had to remind himself to tread carefully. It would be too easy to take her words at face value.

He must not allow himself to forget how he'd fallen for her sincerity before.

Had she been telling the truth on his yacht? Or was she trying to paint herself in a favourable light with him? And if so, for what purpose?

He'd spent seven years telling himself he didn't give a fig for her but the truth was her betrayal had lived in his guts like poison; he could feel it now, uncoiling inside him, the memories of his misplaced faith and trust in her biting into him.

He leaned forward and lowered his voice, trying to read what emotion lay behind the blue eyes staring back at him. 'Why did you choose him over me, Natasha? I always thought it was the money. Was it that? Was it the money and the lifestyle?'

Her hands had balled into fists but there was no fight in her returning stare, just starkness.

His chest rising heavily, Matteo took a large drink of his wine and stared hard at the anguish on her face. He should have ordered something stronger. 'I need to know why. I want to put the past behind us but every time I think I have, something reminds me and it all kicks back in. You strung me along for months…'

Her head shook but her lips stayed stubbornly stuck together.

'Talk to me.' Realising his voice had risen, he strove to lower it again. 'Tell me, Natasha. Make me understand.'

'Look…' She relaxed her hands and took a gulp of her grape juice. Before she could say what she'd intended their meals were brought to the table and laid before them with a flourish.

Natasha looked at her artfully displayed dish and struggled to hold on.

In the space of a minute she'd completely lost her appetite.

Matteo seemed in no rush to eat his food either. He didn't touch his cutlery, just sat there, eyes fixed on her, waiting for her to speak and explain herself.

She couldn't blame him. This conversation had been a long time coming.

She took another drink of her juice. How she wished the grapes had been fermented into wine. It would make this easier.

'I know you don't believe this but everything you and I talked about and the plans we made, I meant it all.'

Natasha knew before the words had finished leaving her mouth that it was the wrong opening gambit.

His eyes narrowed dangerously. 'If you meant any of it then why were you seeing Pieta at the same time? Did you decide to string us both along until you worked out which of us would make the better husband and give you the better lifestyle?'

'Do you want to hear my side or not?'

There was the slightest flare of his nostrils before he inclined his head.

'I didn't string you along for months. The first time Pieta showed any interest in me was at my eighteenth birthday party. I didn't even think he would turn up for it. I assumed a party like that would be beneath him.'

She'd been devastated when Matteo had called to say he'd missed his flight and wouldn't be able to make it. She'd known it wasn't his fault and that his job wasn't one he could drop—his job, back then, had been a case of life or death. So she'd put a brave face on her disappointment and instead turned her calendar over to the following month when they would both be in Pisa for his aunt and uncle's wedding anniversary party, and drew a tiny heart in the corner of that date.

His jaw clenched. 'You strung me along for that long?'

She shook her head. 'I thought he was being polite.'

'Polite?' Disbelief etched itself on his face.

'He was so much older than me...'

'Pieta is—was—the same age as me.'

Her heart twisted to see the pain that flashed over him at the utterance of his best friend's name.

'But I never felt the age gap with you. Pieta was so serious, he came across as older than his years. He took me to the theatre as a birthday present to see a political play. I hate politics. I didn't have the heart to tell him it was the most boring two hours of my life. Maybe if I'd told him the truth he would have seen me differently and things would have turned out differently too but I didn't and things took on a life of their own. He was in England on business and took me out to dinner a couple of times but I swear I didn't think they meant anything...'

'If they didn't mean anything then why didn't you tell me about them?'

'Because it was during the week you went to Washington for that conference. We hardly spoke that week, don't you remember?'

A pulse ticked in his jaw, his lips tightening.

'Pieta took me to these wonderfully grown-up restaurants and spoke about politics and his humanitarian work. I admit, I was overawed by it all. He was this great man making waves across the world for his philanthropy... I was in awe of him and he knew it, but I swear, I never thought of those dates as dates. The first I knew that he was seeing me in a romantic light was when he asked my father's permission to marry me that Friday, two weeks before his parents' anniversary party.'

'He asked your *father*?'

'That was Pieta all over, wasn't it?' She smiled sadly. 'He took his responsibilities very seriously. It wouldn't have occurred to him to ask me for my views first. He saw the awe on my face and interpreted it as infatuation.'

'And your father said yes?'

'Of course he did. He didn't even have to think about it. It was exactly what he wanted. Pieta was rich and connected and had royal blood in his veins. He was the dream son-in-law to brag about down at the golf club.'

'I can understand why your father would have

been keen but that doesn't explain why you went along with it. You could have said no.'

'I did say no.' She squeezed her eyes shut as the memory of her parents' fury played vividly before her eyes. 'My parents knew I was serious about you...'

'Really?' he asked sardonically, finishing his wine.

'Yes! I lived with them, remember? They knew how I felt but they didn't care. They told me to keep my mouth shut about you or I would ruin everything. They told me it was my chance to make them proud after a lifetime of disappointment.'

The scorn in his eyes diminished a little. 'They said that?'

'That and a whole lot of other things too. You had ancient royal blood too but they looked at the wealth Pieta was accumulating, looked at the estate he would inherit and knew that if I married him all their money problems would be over. They were *terribly* in debt. Pieta must have made promises to them because within months of our engagement their debts were gone and he'd paid for them to have an extension put on the house.'

'You agreed to marry him for an extension?' Matteo had picked up his fork and was running his thumb backwards and forwards over the prongs.

'No! That came later. I went along with it because I didn't know what else to do. I wasn't stringing you along, don't you see that? I was playing for time until you got to Pisa for the party and I could tell you to your face what was happening because I couldn't think of a way out.'

'You should have told me as soon as he asked your father's permission.'

'I know that now but at the time I thought it would make things worse. How could I tell you over the phone when you were thousands of miles away that your best friend and cousin wanted to marry me? My head was all over the place. I was only eighteen. I wasn't some cosmopolitan woman with years of experience behind her. I was weak and spineless and I'd got myself backed into a corner I didn't know how to get out of. I wanted desperately to please my parents but at the same time I wanted to be with you. I was waiting for you to get there because I convinced myself you would think of a way out of the mess.'

Natasha took a deep breath and stared at her plate.

Matteo stabbed a roasted shallot with his fork but made no effort to eat it. His eyes were as hard as the tone of his voice. 'You did have the chance to tell me. You made no effort to tell me, remember? But you did let me kiss you.'

She closed her eyes, remembering how she'd taken one look at him in the *castello* and her heart had beaten so hard she'd hardly been able to breathe. After months of increasingly intimate correspondence and phone calls and only a quick snapshot of him on her phone to look at, seeing him in the flesh again…

And then he'd kissed her, their very first kiss— *her* very first kiss—and there had been no breath left to steal. And then Francesca had come barging down the corridor, breaking the moment.

What Natasha hadn't known then was that it had been her last chance to tell Matteo the truth.

CHAPTER SEVEN

NATASHA OPENED HER eyes and forced herself to meet Matteo's unblinking gaze. 'I'm sorry. I thought I'd be able to tell you later that night. I thought I had more time but it was too late. I have kicked myself so many times for not anticipating he would propose publicly like that but I swear I didn't know he was going to do it.'

'Why should I believe you?' he said, not an iota of softening in his stare.

She shrugged helplessly. 'I went to your room in the *castello* that night. I still hoped even then that it wasn't too late for us and that you'd be able to come up with some plan, but you'd gone. I called you but you'd blocked my number—you blocked it that very night. How would I know that if I hadn't tried to call you?'

He *had* blocked her number straight away, Matteo remembered. He'd said goodbye to his family, had managed to force his congratulations to Pieta, walked into the *castello*'s courtyard and into the waiting cab and had immediately blocked her every means of contacting him.

Could she be telling the truth?

'A part of me even hoped you would tell Pieta about us,' she whispered into the bleak silence that had developed between them.

'After he'd publicly proposed and you'd publicly accepted? I would never have humiliated him like that.' He laughed bitterly, his mind reeling from everything she'd confessed.

He looked in the blue eyes that held his. He read the pleading in them.

But what was she pleading for? Forgiveness? Or for him to believe her?

Right then he didn't know what the hell to think or believe.

'You were engaged for six years. You left your parents' home and went to university. You had *six years* to end things with him.'

'When I knew there was no way back with you I decided to stop fighting and just accept it. Accepting it meant pleasing my parents. I told you, back then I was weak and spineless.'

'And you're not now?'

'No.' He saw the defiance bloom in her. 'No. I learned to grow a spine. I had to. And I'm glad I did because it will make me a better mother.' She hung her head and rubbed her temples before looking back at him. 'Just, please, believe my feelings for you were genuine.'

His heart as full as he'd ever known it to be, he nodded slowly. 'Did Pieta ever suspect your feelings for him weren't?'

'Why do you assume his feelings were any more genuine than mine?' Natasha asked before she could stop herself.

'Because he always told me he would know the perfect woman to marry when he found her.'

She clamped down on a burst of her own bitter laughter at the notion. As if her husband had ever looked at her as perfect for anything but the façade he wanted the world to see and the estate he'd wanted to inherit. It didn't matter how hard she'd tried, she'd never been good enough for anyone, not her parents and certainly not her husband.

But she would be good enough for her child and she would do everything in her power to ensure her child never felt that he or she wasn't perfect exactly as they were. She wouldn't diminish them and make them think their best could never be good enough. She would celebrate what they could do and love them regardless of what they couldn't. In short, she would adopt parenting skills at the opposite end of the spectrum to her own parents.

She stared levelly at Matteo. 'I tried very hard to be the best fiancée and then wife that I could be. Do you really think he would have married me if he'd had any doubts?'

Before he could answer, their waitress came to their table and looked at their untouched plates with concern. 'Is everything all right with your food?'

Like a switch had been turned on, Matteo bestowed on her his dazzling smile. 'Everything's great, thanks.'

Smiling, she bustled away.

The interruption had been what they needed.

When Natasha looked at him again he sighed deeply, his eyes boring into her but without the animosity of before.

'We should eat before it gets cold,' he said, finally popping the shallot into his mouth, his tone leaving no doubt that, as far as he was concerned, the conversation was over.

He'd got the answers he was seeking. Whether he believed them or not, she had no control over.

What difference did it make now, in any case? Whatever their feelings had been for each other, it was in the past and it had to stay in the past.

Matteo knocked on the guesthouse door. A minute later Natasha opened it, dressed in a pair of red pyjama bottoms and a black vest. Her usually sleek hair had an unkempt look about it.

She greeted him with one of the smiles that always pierced him in so many different ways.

'I wasn't expecting to see you today,' she said, standing aside to let him in.

'I had a conference call with my clinic managers. We were done sooner than I thought we'd be. Have I woken you?' It was approaching midday.

'I was reading.' She held up the book in her hand. It was a pregnancy book the obstetrician had given her.

'I thought you'd already read that.'

She shrugged. 'No harm in reading it again and there isn't much else for me to do.'

'That's why I'm here.'

'Oh?'

'Have you eaten?'

'What is it with you and my eating habits?' she asked, the trace of a smile playing on her lips.

'I like to be sure you're taking care of yourself. Have you?'

'I had breakfast a couple of hours ago.'

'Then get dressed. I'm taking you out to lunch.'

There was a definite brightening in her eyes. 'Give me twenty minutes. I need to shower.'

He bit back the offer he wanted to make of joining her in it, instead taking a seat at the dining table, following her retreating figure with his eyes. The pyjama bottoms emphasised her bottom, showing its rounded peachy shape beautifully.

He closed his eyes and rubbed his temples.

Since their meal at Key Biscayne ten days ago things had changed between them. It had been a subtle shift but one he felt in his marrow.

He'd gone over her words from that night many times. As hard as it was to override seven years of conditioned loathing towards her, the more he thought about it the more he believed her.

What disturbed him was how much he *wanted* to believe her, and not just because she was carrying his child.

He looked at her now, seven years older, and saw all the things that had been missing before. She *had* been mature beyond her years but it was only now that he was with the fully grown-up Natasha that he realised her maturity back then hadn't been that of a rounded woman with life experience under her belt. She'd been a wide-eyed innocent, blooming as she'd embraced womanhood, excited for her future and what it held. She'd also been a people-pleaser. She'd been almost desperate to please, never giving contrary thoughts or opinions. He remembered how delighted he'd been to find someone so like-minded but now he realised she would have agreed with his tastes and likes whatever they had been.

They'd spent more time together these past ten days. She had no qualms about giving her opinion now and although her tastes did concur a great deal with his own, she never hesitated to voice her own thoughts when they disagreed.

He'd taken her out to dinner a handful of times and to the theatre to watch a musical adaptation of a popular film. She'd clapped along all the way through it. When he'd asked her opinion at the end she'd said that she'd loved it but had wanted to gag the leading lady for her annoying voice.

She was far more interesting now. And somehow more desirable for it, which he hadn't thought possible. He would gaze at her creamy skin and remember how it had felt beneath his fingers. He would look at the honey-blonde hair and remember how it had felt brushed against his shoulder. He would look in the blue eyes and remember the look in them when she'd come with him buried deep inside her.

And he would remember that slight resistance of her body when he'd first thrust inside her and how he'd felt a warning shoot through his head that had been drowned out by the passion of her kisses and the ardour of her response.

If he didn't know better, he would have said that resistance had been the natural resistance of a body unused to being made love to. Which wasn't possible.

But it still nagged at him, playing in his mind like a distant but nearing wind, and though they'd both made a concerted effort not to speak of Pieta or the past since that first meal out, it was there too, hanging between them like a basket of dead flowers.

Until he'd brought Natasha to Miami everything had been cut and dried. He knew who she was and what she'd done. He knew who he was and what he'd done.

Now he was discovering that all his certainties were whispers in that nearing wind and the only thing with any substance to it was his desire for her. It was with him all the time, a constant thickening of his blood, a constant charge in his skin.

When she reappeared thirty minutes later wearing a white summer dress with strappy sleeves and a pair of flat roman sandals, her hair damp around her shoulders, her perfume filling the room as vibrantly as she did just by her presence, he felt the air escape his lungs.

Dio, was there nothing this woman wore that didn't make him want to rip it off?

He got to his feet, keeping his loins under control by the skin of his teeth. 'Ready to go?'

'Where to?' she asked.

'Downtown.'

Natasha strapped herself into the small sports car Matteo had chosen to drive from his vast collection while he pressed the button to put the roof down. The engine started at the press of another button, music pumped out and then he was driving them out of his garage, out of his estate and through the wide open streets of the exclusive gated community he lived in. Soon the verdant verges thick with trees thinned, the large, mostly hidden homes became buildings that steadily increased in height, and the open road filled with traffic.

Downtown turned out to be a thriving metropolis full of character and colour and all kinds of scents. Her hair whipped around her face which with the sun shining down on them acted as an industrial hairdryer.

He drove them round the back of a gleaming skyscraper that looked over the harbour and into the underground car park, coming to a stop in a space with his name on it.

'Handy,' she commented. 'Are these your offices?'

He grinned. 'I need to pop in for a few minutes to sign some documents before we eat.'

There was an elevator a short walk from the parking space. Matteo punched a code and the doors pinged open. Inside, he pressed the button with the number thirty on it.

'Why did you use a code?' she asked.

'It's a security measure. If you don't know the access code the elevators won't work for you. This is an exclusive elevator for my staff and patients.'

They arrived at their floor before she'd even registered the elevator moving.

The medicinal smell hit her the moment the doors opened.

'Do you do surgery here?' she asked in surprise.

'Where did you think I would do it?'

'Not on the top of a skyscraper. I thought these were your administrative headquarters.'

'They're on the next two floors up.'

'But you run your clinic in a skyscraper?'

He laughed. 'Trust me, the facilities here are second to none.'

Three receptionists dressed in white clinical uniforms manned the immaculately clean room with the fabulous views of the ocean they stepped into. Matteo had a brief chat with them while Natasha stared around in wonder at the plush furnishings and tasteful artwork.

It was like being in a hospital that had amalgamated with a five-star hotel.

'I can give you a quick tour if you want?'

'As long as you're not going to give me the hard sell for a buttock enhancement or a new nose,' she jested.

The amusement that had played on his lips since the exhilarating drive over faded. It faded from his eyes too, his stare unfathomable. 'You're the last person who needs anything done.'

It was his tone. The starkness to it. It made her veins heat and her chest fill with a longing that made her yearn to reach out and touch him.

That was all she seemed to want to do. Touch him. And smell him.

She could almost believe he meant it. Almost. But she knew too well that something in her did need fixing. Why else had she never pleased her parents in anything she did? Why else would Pieta have chosen her? She'd been wrong for him in every sense possible but still it had been her he'd chosen to be his wife. It had been her he'd trapped into staying with him even after the truth had come out between them.

She didn't want to think about Pieta.

Since her talk with Matteo ten days ago things had been better between them. They'd both made a concerted effort to build bridges without saying so in words. Like so much between them, it wasn't something that needed saying.

What also didn't need to be said was the re-igniting of the chemistry that had always been there, swirling between them but now gaining an intensity she was finding harder to resist.

Resist she must. There was too much danger in it. She'd been besotted by Matteo as a teenager but she wasn't a teenager any more. She was an adult with a little life growing inside her that needed her protection. Learning to find her own voice and not be afraid to speak it had been hard, finding her spine and the courage to stand up for herself harder. She couldn't afford to lose that.

She didn't want to be so vulnerable again. She *couldn't* be. Not for herself and especially not for her baby.

So she swallowed the emotions pushing through her chest and up her throat at the way Matteo was staring at her and forced her tone to be airy as she said, 'I thank you for the compliment but I've always fancied a new nose.'

'Your nose is perfect.'

'Hardly. How about new breasts? We could do a deal—buy one boob, get one free?'

His expression changed, a wryness spreading

over his features, as if he too was pulling himself back. 'I think being pregnant has already done that for you.'

The strange almost melancholic moment broken, he led her down a wide corridor and briskly said, 'I can't show you everything as we have patients in residence and surgeries being performed, but I can show you enough so you get a good feel for what we do here. After all, it will be our child who will inherit it all one day.'

'I hadn't thought of it like that,' she said, startled.

'Once everything's out in the open with the family I'll get a new will drawn up.'

'Really? So soon?'

'Death has no favourites. It can strike anyone at any time.' She knew from the look he gave her that it wasn't the patients he'd dealt with during his residency years he was thinking of but Pieta. 'With us being unmarried I want the peace of mind to know that if anything happens to me, our child will automatically inherit without any protracted legal drama. You should get one done too. We should both do everything we can to protect our child.'

'Okay,' she agreed, knowing it made sense, unbelievably touched at what he planned.

He'd said since the scan that he accepted paternity but his talk about a DNA test, although said in the heat of the moment and soon disregarded, had put doubts in her mind. Only small doubts, but they'd been there, tapping away at her.

This simple deed put those doubts to rest and she could hardly credit the relief sweeping through her.

If this didn't prove he accepted paternity then nothing did.

He believed her.

'We'll have to think about guardians should anything happen to both of us,' he said.

'You have given this a lot of thought.'

'I'm not prepared to leave our child's future to chance.' He pulled a tablet out of his pocket and pressed away at it, saying, 'These are the private rooms the patients stay in post-op.' He put the tablet back in his pocket and opened a door halfway up. 'This one's empty.'

Natasha looked inside. It was like no hospital room she'd ever seen. This was a plush hotel room except more clinically clean.

'Any thoughts on guardians?' he asked, closing the door and leading them on to the end of the corridor. Matteo entered a code into a silver box by the end door. It swung open and they stepped into another corridor with a very different feel to the one they'd just been in. The thick carpets had been replaced with shiny hard flooring, the soft hues of the walls now brilliant white.

'I don't know. If I thought Francesca wasn't going to disown the pair of us, I'd say her.' She only just managed to stop her voice from cracking.

'She might surprise us.'

'Do you really think so?'

'No.'

She sighed. 'Nor do I. We'll have to see how things go and then decide. But definitely not my parents.'

The grimace he gave showed he felt exactly the same way. 'Do they know you're here?'

'No. I haven't spoken to them since the funeral.

They know how to contact me if they want anything.'

He stopped walking abruptly. 'They haven't called you?'

'No. I'm sure they'll crawl out of the woodwork when they think Pieta's inheritance has been sorted. In fairness, I haven't called them either.'

His jaw clenched and he breathed heavily. 'Fairness be damned. You don't owe them anything.'

'I owe them my life,' she pointed out, her heart twisting to see the protective anger on his face. She wanted to stroke that face. She wanted to feel those firm lips on hers again. She wanted it so badly it was becoming like a drug.

Sometimes when they talked she would see more glimpses of the man she'd fallen for all those years ago. Her desire for him then had had such purity to it. Her desire had been innocent, a longing to be with him, to be held by him.

'Anyone can create a life,' he said, his voice low, his face edging towards hers. 'We've proved that. It's how you care for the life once you have it that shows the person you are.'

Almost hypnotised by the intensity in his eyes,

she felt her face inching closer to his in turn, her lids becoming heavy, moisture filling her mouth as the electricity of anticipation danced over her skin.

There was no purity to her desire now. She'd lost her innocence long before she'd lost her virginity. Now her desire was a living thing inside her that fed on his presence, a battle she fought harder with every day that passed.

She wanted him. She craved him. She couldn't bear to fall into bed with him again and when it was over for him to roll over and swear at the horror of what they'd done. For her own sanity she needed to keep a lid on her feelings for him but it was becoming harder as each hour with him prised it off a little more.

Because what she needed to remember more than anything else was that they had no future together as anything other than parents of their child. She'd had one disastrous marriage and couldn't contemplate another relationship.

Matteo didn't want a relationship with her any more than she wanted one with him. That did nothing to stop the chemistry between them taking on its own life form. That did nothing to stop her lips parting and her eyes closing as the whisper of his breath played over her skin and his scent played in her senses...

A loud bang jerked her back to reality as the large swinging doors they'd almost reached were slammed open.

Natasha stepped back and swallowed hard, managing a wan smile at the two medics who strolled past them, greeting Matteo loudly as they passed.

He ran a hand through his dark cropped hair and stilled for a moment before going through the doors that had only just stopped swinging.

'This is our operating wing,' he said in a gruff voice, resuming the tour. He reached again for his tablet, which she realised through the daze their almost kiss had put her in had all the information he needed about what was happening at that very moment in his clinic delivered to his fingertips. 'We have operating theatres and recovery rooms, everything you'd expect from a normal, functioning hospital.' As he spoke, a nurse in full scrubs walked past talking on a phone and waved at them.

'We leave nothing to chance,' Matteo continued. 'Room seven's empty. You can look from the doorway but I must ask you not to go inside. No one's admitted without scrubs on.'

He opened a door for her.

Natasha peered inside and gaped. This was an honest-to-goodness operating theatre, just like those she'd seen on the television. Except bigger. And shinier.

'I need to sign some papers off in my office and then we'll go and eat. How do you like the idea of eating by the docks?'

She strove to match the casual tone he'd now adopted, to pretend that they hadn't nearly just locked lips. To pretend her mouth didn't still tingle and her limbs didn't feel weak with longing for him. 'As long as a seagull doesn't try and steal my chips.'

'You want chips?'

She was glad to think of something that didn't involve his hands running all over her body. 'Yes.

A big bag of chips. And a big American club sandwich.'

'Then that is what you shall have.'

They were back in the reception area, heading up a different corridor. The door at the end had Matteo's name on it.

He unlocked it and she followed him inside.

Like the rest of the clinic, his office was scrupulously clean.

'Do you see clients in here?' she asked, looking around, keen to look anywhere but at him, not when her heart was still pounding beneath her ribs.

'Those that I take on personally, yes.'

'Do you perform many surgeries yourself?'

'Not as many as I used to do. The business has gotten so big it takes all my time. I make sure I do enough to keep my skills sharp.'

He sat behind his desk and pulled a stack of papers from a tray. 'This should only take me ten minutes. Help yourself to coffee—there's decaf if you want it.'

She could sense him avoiding her gaze as much as she was avoiding his.

'I'm good, thanks.'

Needing to keep her gaze away from him, Natasha passed the time by looking round his office, at the shelves crammed with medical texts, the walls lined with his qualification certificates. His certificate from medical school still bore the name Matteo Pellegrini.

She hesitated before asking something she knew had been a majorly important decision in his life. 'Why did you change your surname?'

CHAPTER EIGHT

FROM THE CORNER of her eye Natasha saw the nib of Matteo's pen hover over a sheet before he pressed it down and signed it, then placed it on the fresh pile he was making. 'Because I no longer wished to be acknowledged as my father's son.'

'It got that bad?' Their relationship had never been the same since the childhood fire that had ruined both little boys' lives.

'Don't pretend you don't know, *bella*. I'm sure you were told all the details.'

'Are you talking about the argument you two had at your brother's funeral?'

He jerked a nod and signed another form.

Pieta had asked her to go to Roberto's funeral with him. It had been one of the only times she'd ever denied him anything he'd asked of her. She'd stood her ground doggedly, pointing out she'd never met Roberto and that seeing as it was going to be such a small, intimate funeral, it would be inappropriate for her to be there. Pieta hadn't wanted her there for support—he hadn't seen Roberto in years—he'd wanted her there for appearances' sake. Even back then she'd known that. Appearances be damned, she'd thought; she wouldn't put Matteo through it. He would have hated to see her there. It would have made a bad day even more difficult for him.

Thinking back on it, her refusal had been the moment she'd discovered that she did have a spine. She'd found it for Matteo's sake.

'I know you two had a blazing row and that you changed your surname two weeks later. I never knew what the argument was about but I assumed the two events were linked.'

'You assumed? You never asked Pieta?'

'I never asked about you, not to him or anyone. Any news I heard about you came about in general conversation.'

Slowly he turned his head to look at her, his green eyes narrowed.

She raised her shoulders and pulled her lips

in before saying quietly, 'I had this fear that if I brought your name up, they'd be able to see through me.'

'What did you think they'd see?'

'The truth about our past.'

And the truth that my feelings for you ran deeper than anything I tried to feel for Pieta.

'Eventually it stopped mattering, but not speaking about you became a habit.'

He stared at her for a long time, so hard it was like he was trying to dig into her mind. Eventually he sighed and dragged a hand down his face. 'At the funeral my father said it should have been me he was burying, not Roberto.'

Her mouth dropped open, utter shock thumping her.

'Seriously? He said that to you?'

'Sì.'

'That's *outrageous*. My God, Matteo, I'm so sorry. It must have been the grief talking—he couldn't have meant it.' How could a father say such a thing to a child? Her parents had manipulated her and twisted her emotions to suit their own purposes but never had they wished her dead.

Something sharp clawed into her chest, over-long talons scraping through her heart, making it bleed to imagine what it must have been like for Matteo to bury the brother he loved with one breath and then in the next to hear his own father say he wished him dead.

How could someone be so cruel?

'He meant it. He never forgave me for the fire. I always knew in my heart that he blamed me for it and at the funeral he confirmed it.' Matteo could still hear his father's words in his ear and feel the spittle that had flown from his mouth as he'd delivered his hate-filled words.

They'd buried Roberto under blue skies and warm sunshine, the kind of glorious day his brother had loved for the first eight years of his life but had shunned for the last twenty. He'd hated people seeing the horrific burn scars that had covered his body. He'd refused to look in mirrors, would refuse to enter a room if it had reflective surfaces in it. He'd shunned everyone who wasn't immediate family, only leaving the house for medical purposes. He'd lost all his love for life and become a recluse.

Matteo had said goodbye to his brother, his heart bursting that Roberto's last journey should be so blessed with such glorious weather, grabbing hold of any sign of blessing he could to ease the pain racking him.

Then, as he'd turned from the graveside, his father had snatched hold of his arm and spilled his venom all over him.

'That's *rubbish*.' Natasha looked like she was about to burst into tears, her face white, her eyes glistening. 'How could it be your fault?'

'I was in charge of him when it happened.'

'You were *ten years old*.'

Somehow Natasha's outrage and upset warmed the coldness that had filled his core as it always did when he remembered that dreadful day.

'I know how young I was and it took a long time for me to accept the blame wasn't mine. It didn't—doesn't—stop the guilt,' he told her slowly. 'Deep down I always knew my father blamed me too and that it was the root cause of our estrangement. I spent twenty years hoping for his forgiveness. I always hoped he would see what I was doing with medicine and be proud of me. I always dreamed of the day he would welcome me back into the fold.' The bitter laugh escaped his mouth again. 'I learned at Roberto's funeral that I would never get it.'

'But *why*? I don't understand. How can he blame you? You were a *child*.' Fat tears shone in her eyes.

Those tears were for him…

Inhaling deeply, he said, 'He left a wilful ten-year-old boy in charge of a wilful eight-year-old. My parents left their two children on their own so they could enjoy a nice long lunch with their friends. To forgive me means accepting his own responsibility for the fire. He lies to himself about it every single day. He's lied to himself now for twenty-five years. He would rather lose two sons than accept his own part of the blame, so if he wishes me dead then to hell with him. When he said what he did at the graveside…something in me snapped. Roberto was gone…there was nothing to keep me there any longer. My last link with my parents was gone. I decided that if I'm not his son and he wished me dead then he didn't deserve for me to have his name.'

'But what about your mother?' she asked with a bewildered shake of her head, her words low and ragged. 'Didn't it upset her when you changed your name?'

'My aunt Vanessa was more of a mother to me than mine ever was and she wasn't even blood. My mother was no better than my father. She allowed me to visit Roberto when my father was away on business but she never stood up for me or insisted, as was her right, that I be allowed back to live in the family home. I was her first born and she washed her hands of me just as he did. Like my father she dishonestly put the blame on me rather than accept her own part in it. So I chose my aunt's maiden name. It felt fitting.'

The tears poured down Natasha's face, her shoulders shaking. Then, so quickly he barely registered her move, she was by his side and taking his face in her trembling hands. She pressed her lips tightly to his, not as a kiss of passion but one that had a clinging desperation to it, her tears splashing onto his cheeks.

Before he could respond or react in any way, she broke away and punched his shoulder, fury now mingling with the distress. 'How could you give it all up?'

'What?' Her sudden turnaround of both conversation and mood had him reeling.

'Your dreams.' She wiped her face furiously but the tears kept coming. 'Your plans to do reconstructive surgery. You keep saying you didn't give it up and only changed career paths but you *did*. You gave up everything you'd worked for. I know you could never have helped your brother surgically but you wanted to help others in the same situation. You *did*. You were so driven and dedicated. It was never about the money for you.' She raised her hands and waved them, taking in the luxury furnishings and the spectacular view he enjoyed. 'It was never about *this*.'

He didn't know what cut through his skin the most, her scornful words or the distress behind them. Both stunned him as much as her tears. Somehow he managed to hold onto his rising temper. 'I wanted to be a surgeon—I *am* a surgeon.'

'A surgeon with his own Jetstream, a yacht and

the most expensive property in Miami. You followed the money. Was it to prove a point to your father when being the most brilliant doctor in a generation wasn't enough? You would have been brilliant. I know you would. You had everything there and you threw it away for money.'

'I didn't throw anything away,' he snarled, getting to his feet and kicking his chair back. 'I paid my dues. You know how hard I worked to get through medical school and my residency. I spent over a decade working so hard that there were days I never saw sunlight. I never shirked in my duty, not even when I couldn't feel my feet from standing for so long or when I had to drink gallons of coffee just to keep my eyes open. Yes, I followed the money but so what? Only a fool wouldn't. I developed the lotion for Roberto but it was too bloody late for him. His scarred lungs gave up on him. *Everything* I did was for him but he died, so what was the point? What was the point in working every waking hour when I had nothing to show for it apart from certificates to hang on my wall?

'I saw an opportunity with the lotion to create a

skincare range that worked, and I took it. I make no apologies for that. The money I made from it allowed me to open my own clinics, which made me even more money. I've worked my backside off for years so why shouldn't I be allowed to enjoy it? I'm richer than I ever dreamed possible and, yes, it gives me *immense* satisfaction to think of my father knowing of my wealth and not being able to claim any credit for it because I threw away the name he gave me.'

Stark silence fell between them.

Somehow during his vehement rebuttal they'd finished barely a foot apart, close enough for Matteo to see the exact shade of red slowly creeping up Natasha's neck and over her cheeks.

Her tears had dried up and now she simply stared at him with wide eyes that held his for the longest time before a flash of pain raced through them.

Her throat moved before she whispered, 'I'm sorry. I should never have said any of that. I don't know what got into me.'

'Never apologise for speaking the truth. It might hurt but lies are always, *always* worse.'

He looked at the light smattering of freckles over the bridge of her nose and brought his face lower to hers, remembering the feel of her lips on his before the torrent had spewed from her.

He'd never known such passion before. He'd had a steady string of women in his life over the years, pleasant interludes in a busy life, a pretty face to be photographed with when he opened a new clinic and used the media for publicity...

Natasha was right that part of what had driven him had been to prove a point to his father. That *had* been conscious, striving to achieve the riches his father had never been able to find, but it was only at that moment he understood there had been another driving force propelling him forward too.

Her.

Every photo posed for knowing it would be all over the media had been taken with *her* image in his head. She had been with him of every minute of every day, living in his subconscious, the woman who'd thrown away a future that could have been special for them to be with his richer cousin. And only now, years later, did he realise he no longer believed any of it.

He believed her. He believed right down in his soul that she'd spoken the truth when she'd explained how it had been for her. It had never been about the money for her.

'Seven years ago you kept the truth from me,' he said, running a thumb over her cheekbone, unable to tear his gaze from those beautiful blue eyes. 'If you'd found your voice before it was too late who knows how our lives would have turned out? Maybe we would have married each other. Maybe we would have naturally drifted apart. Neither of us can know.'

Leaning to rest the tip of his nose against hers, he continued, 'We're having a child together, *bella*. I might not have liked what you just said but you've found your voice and have learned how to use it, and you can't know how good that is. I spent too many years distrusting and hating you—I don't ever want to return to feeling like that. For better or worse we're going to be tied together by our child for the rest of our lives and the only way we're going to get through it is by always being honest with each other. We will argue and disagree but you must always speak the truth to me.'

Natasha fought to keep her feet grounded and her limbs from turning into fondue but it was a fight she was losing, Matteo's breath warm on her face, his thumb gently moving on her skin but scorching it, the heat from his body almost penetrating her clothes, heat crawling through her, pooling in her most intimate place.

His scent was right there too, filling every part of her, and she wanted to bury her nose into his neck and inhale him.

She'd kissed him without any thought, a desperate compulsion to touch him and comfort him flooding her, and then the fury had struck from nowhere, all her private thoughts about the direction he'd taken his career in converging to realise he'd thrown it all away in the pursuit of riches.

And now she wanted to kiss him again.

As if he could sense the need inside her, he brought his mouth close to hers but not quite touching, the promise of a kiss.

'And now I will ask you something and I want

complete honesty,' he whispered, the movement of his words making his lips dance against hers like a breath.

The fluttering of panic sifted into the compulsive desire. She hated lies too. She never wanted to tell another, especially not to him. But she had to keep her wits about her because there were things she just could not tell because no matter what he said about lies always being worse, sometimes it was the truth that could destroy a life.

But, God, how could she think properly when her head was turning into candyfloss at his mere touch?

His other hand trailed down her back and clasped her bottom to pull her flush to him. Her abdomen clenched to feel his erection pressing hard against her lower stomach. His lips moved lightly over hers, still tantalising her with the promise of his kiss. 'Do you want me to let you go?'

Her hands that she'd clenched into fists at her sides to stop from touching him back unfurled themselves and inched to his hips.

The hand stroking her cheek moved round her head and speared her hair. 'Tell me.' His lips found her exposed neck and nipped gently at it. 'Do you want me to stop?'

'Matteo...' Finally, she found her voice.

'Yes, *bella*?'

'Don't stop.'

Her words were all the encouragement he needed. His mouth swept across her cheek to find her parted lips and then he was kissing her with such hunger she melted into him.

The fuse relit in an instant. Need burned bright within her, all the desire she'd been suppressing by the skin of her fingers bursting out of her. She wrapped her arms tightly around his waist, her hands reaching up to clasp onto his back as she kissed him back, her tongue darting into his mouth, dancing against his.

And he held her just as tightly. One hand buried in her hair, the other gripping her to him, devouring her as if her kisses were the air he needed to breathe.

When he broke it and let go of her she almost cried a protest but then he took her face in his hands and rubbed both thumbs across her cheek-bones as he stared intently into her eyes. 'I'm not making love to you here.'

Love...?

Although she knew his words weren't meant in the terms of what love itself meant, something in her heart broke free regardless, taking all the air from her lungs.

Only when she'd found her breath did she whisper, 'Then take me home.'

The drive back to Matteo's home passed in a blur. What had been a relatively short journey into downtown seemed to halve, Matteo driving his powerful car to the limit, weaving in and out of the traffic, his jaw clenched, his focus very much on the road before them. Only his right hand, holding hers tightly on her lap as he navigated the roads, showed any awareness of her beside him.

When he pulled into the garage what felt like only minutes later, Natasha shook her head, amazed to find she could remember nothing about the drive. All she'd been able to focus on was their kiss, replaying it in her head, her lips still tingling, her body still experiencing the hard pressure of his body pressed against her as if he'd imprinted himself on her.

As soon as he stopped the car, Matteo leaned over and kissed her again, a deep, heady kiss that sent her head spinning all over again.

'*Dio, bella*, you're driving me out of my mind,' he muttered into her mouth before pulling away to get out of the car.

On legs that felt as if they were new born, Natasha stepped out too. He was by her side in an instant, taking her hand and leading her up the steps of the garage and into the empty house.

She'd never been upstairs and where before she'd wondered a lot about what she would find there, she now found she didn't care, not even when she followed him up the hidden staircase. All she could see at that moment was Matteo. She refused to think about anything else.

But then they stepped into his bedroom and she gasped at the beauty and simplicity of it. It was so *clean* but without being clinical, huge without being oppressive and bathed in light that softened the high walls and gave it such a romantic feel that she felt her belly melt all over again.

She looked at Matteo to find his gaze very much on her, his jaw clenched as it had been during the drive back.

Stepping to him, she reached up to palm his cheek and stare at the face she'd adored for so many years it seemed she'd gone to sleep with it in her mind every night for ever.

He breathed deeply before reaching out to gently brush a fallen lock of her hair away from her eyes.

It was at that moment she realised she'd never got over losing him.

The pain she'd felt when hearing of his father's rejection and wish for Matteo to have been the son that had died had cut as deep as if it had been personally directed at her. Whatever choices Matteo had made with his life since they'd dreamed of building a future together all those years ago, it didn't change that fundamentally he was the best man she'd ever known.

He was the father of her child and she couldn't

have chosen a better man for it if she'd been given a list with a thousand names on it.

Was this love? she wondered, dazed at the notion. Or was it just hormones from the pregnancy and a strong case of lust? Whatever it was, the need inside her for him was too strong to even want to fight it any more, not when the green eyes staring back at her were molten with his own unmistakable desire.

And then he hooked an arm around her waist and pulled her flush against him and his hot mouth was back on hers and they were kissing as if they could feed from the other.

Their lovemaking the night they'd conceived their child had been born of a passion fuelled by pain and anger, an old longing that had been kept locked away, out of sight and mind, only to erupt with vengeance at the first opportunity.

This time, as Matteo lifted her into his strong arms to carry her to the bed, the flames had lit to burn as brightly as they had then but this time there was a sense of wonder and a complete sense of rightness.

In a melee of arms and legs, he laid her down,

just as he had before but with a tenderness beneath the passion.

When he kissed her, it was with a slow, tempered hunger that was only broken when his hands found the hem of her dress and he pulled it up to take it off her, then smoothed her dislodged hair before kissing her again.

Raking her hands into his short curly hair, Natasha sighed as his lips trailed down her neck, shivered as they brushed over her collarbone.

He bent his head lower, reaching her sensitive breasts that were already much heavier than the last time they'd made love. Kissing each one over her lacy bra, he rested his chin between them and looked at her. 'You're beautiful, you know that, *bella*?'

She swallowed, not wanting to think of all the beautiful women she'd seen him photographed with over the years.

'I mean it.' There was an intensity in his eyes that matched the intensity in his voice. 'No one can hold a candle to you.'

Matteo saw the doubt flicker in her eyes and wondered what Natasha saw when she looked in the mirror. He remembered her jests earlier in his clinic, words said, he knew, to detract from the spell that had woven around them, but there had been something underlying it.

Did she really not see how beautiful she was? Did she really not know that just listening to her voice was enough for his loins to tighten?

Raising himself up, he climbed off the bed and stripped his shirt off and divested himself of the rest of his clothes, her eyes following his every movement.

Only when he was naked did he get back on the bed and trail his fingers from her neck all the way to the line of her knickers, delighting in the way she quivered at his touch.

There was such innocence in her responses that he found hard to get his head around. On the one hand her responses were ardent, her need and hunger for him as visible and as open as a man could wish for, but now, gazing at the almost naked form of the woman he'd dreamed about for years in the hazy daylight, he could believe he was the first man to have ever seen her like this.

Placing a hand behind her back, he lifted her so

he could undo the pretty bra hiding her breasts from him. As the lacy material loosened to free her, she tilted her head back and sighed.

The first time they'd made love had been in the dark. Now he could see her perfectly and she was even more perfect than he had imagined. Had her nipples always been that dark or was that the pregnancy working its magic in her?

Dipping his head, he took one into his mouth, eliciting another sigh from her.

As he'd done the first time, he kissed every inch of her, but this time he took it slowly. He wanted to savour it, savour her, to learn everything about her that he could, to find the zones that provoked the loudest gasps and the sharpest digs of her nails into his skin. When he hooked a finger to the side of her knickers, she wriggled beneath him, helping him pull them down her thighs and legs before he threw them with the rest of their discarded clothes onto the floor.

The heat he found in her most feminine part blew his mind and when he brushed over the soft hair and rubbed a thumb over the centre of her pleasure, her eyes widened and a moan flew from her mouth. Keeping a steady pressure with his thumb, he slowly slid a finger into the damp heat. She moaned again and arched her back, her hair falling like a waterfall onto the pillow.

Dio, he had never known anything like this. He could make love to her for ever.

He kissed the softly rounded belly then kissed lower to replace his thumb with his tongue, inhaling the musky sweetness he would gladly bottle and keep on him always.

Her little sighs of pleasure deepened and she whispered his name. Before he could finish what he'd started she wriggled beneath him and sat up, pouncing on him so she straddled him, her arms locked around his neck and her hands cradling his scalp as she fused her lips to his with a hunger that sucked the air from him.

Then she touched and kissed him everywhere, just as he had done to her, his shoulders, his arms, his stomach, his thighs, his aching erection, her mouth leaving a trail of heat on his skin that fired his blood to a level he'd never imagined. And in the fever with which she so beautifully caressed him was a reverence, almost as if she were exploring him with wonder in her heart side by side with the passion that drove them both.

He felt his flesh could burst open to admit her into *his* heart.

Gripping her waist, he manoeuvred them both so she straddled his lap and her legs were wrapped around his waist.

Their lips locked together, he placed a hand flat on her back and laid her back gently, the tip of his burning arousal finding the place it so badly needed to be. Then he entered her, slowly, tenderly until he was burrowed deep inside her tight heat.

The sensations that enveloped him threatened to make him come in an instant and he had to grit his teeth to keep himself in check. Only when he was certain he had himself under control did he start moving.

But, *Dio*, every long thrust built the sensation up to unimaginable levels, every moan and pant from her lips, every scratch of her nails, all combined to make him lose himself in the rapture that was Natasha.

Only when the moans breathing into his mouth

deepened and the hand holding onto his buttock gripped tightly and he felt her thicken around him did he finally let himself go with a groan that came from the very centre of his being, plunging so deeply into her that he no longer knew where he ended and she began.

When the explosive pulsations inside him had dulled to a gentle buzz he shifted his weight a little so as not to crush her.

Immediately her arms tightened around him and she raised her face to bury it in his neck.

'If you regret what we just did tell me now so I can prepare myself before I have to look at you again,' she whispered into his skin.

His chest contorting to remember how he'd reacted in the immediate aftermath of their first time together, he held her securely in his arms and rolled onto his back, taking her with him. 'No regrets,' he whispered back, stroking her hair.

How could he regret that? Something that special could never be looked on with regret.

Her small hand groped for his and squeezed

and she nuzzled into his chest with a sigh. 'I don't regret it either.'

'Good.' He brought her hand to his lips to kiss it. 'No regrets.'

'No regrets,' she echoed.

CHAPTER NINE

THEY STAYED IN bed until the sun began its descent. They'd made love again and, just as she drifted off, he asked if she was hungry. The mention of hunger was enough to make Natasha's stomach growl and remind her that they'd skipped the lunch he'd promised her.

He laughed and got out of bed. What looked like an ordinary wall had turned out to be a walk-in wardrobe. He disappeared into it, reappearing with a pair of tan shorts on, leaned over to kiss her firmly and said he was going to call a chef from the staff quarters to make them something.

Happy to have a few minutes alone to relive every beautiful moment in her head, Natasha burrowed her face into his pillow seeking his scent.

Making love to Matteo the first time had been

an explosion that had detonated itself. This time it had been…

It had been incredible. He'd been so passionate and yet so tender. There had been a connection between them she could never have put into words but it filled her heart with such hope.

But hopes of what? A future together? Him and her and baby makes three?

She grabbed his pillow and pulled it over her head.

One incredible afternoon in bed together did not make a future. It just made complications and there were enough complications in her life for her to be getting on with.

That didn't stop her waiting impatiently for his return.

When twenty minutes passed without him coming back to the room, concern began to nibble at her. Fishing in the pile of discarded clothes for her dress, she slipped it over her head, intent on searching for him. But no sooner had she stepped out of the room than apprehension suddenly suffused her.

What if he'd left the bedroom and become

filled with recriminations again? What if she'd been lying in his bed waiting for his return while he'd been overcome with angry remorse and was trying to think of a way to kick her out and back to the guesthouse?

What if she'd been lying on his bed feeling that she'd slipped into a blissful dream and he'd come to the conclusion that he'd slipped into a nightmare?

She found him in the vast living space she'd been so enamoured with in her first visit there. He was sitting at the table, his long legs stretched out before him, talking on his phone.

He gave an apologetic smile and held out a hand to her.

Her relief was almost dizzying.

It was also terrifying.

She let her fingers drift to touch his and took the seat beside him, her heart thumping madly, her palms suddenly clammy.

Making love like they had had changed every-thing.

His eyes fixed on her, he continued his conver-sation, his Italian too rapid-fire for her to keep up. She'd never mastered the language, another regret in her life. It had such a beautiful cadence to it and in the days when she and Matteo had been planning a future together, she'd imagined him teaching her his language.

It had never occurred to her to ask Pieta.

When the call was over, Matteo put his phone on the table. 'That was Daniele. He wants to go back to Caballeros with me at the end of next week.'

She closed her eyes. All the euphoria of their lovemaking, which even her panic about Matteo finding regrets hadn't been able to fully quash, left her. 'Next week? And we'll go to Pisa after?'

'Yes. Next Friday. I'll charter a plane for you and meet you there. It makes more sense than me flying back to Miami to collect you.'

Natasha felt the panic welling up in her and fought hard to stifle it. 'At least that gives us almost two weeks to prepare. Do you think he has any suspicions about us yet?'

Saying the word 'us' felt different from all the other times she'd said it. This time it felt real.

'Daniele takes things at face value so I doubt it.'

She mustered a smile. 'I never got to know him that well. Not like I did Francesca and Vanessa.'

'You're speaking of them in the past tense.'

She met his eyes. 'When they learn about us and the baby my relationship with them will be in the past.'

'Yes. And so will mine.' His admission was like a long, drawn out sigh but then he leaned forward in his chair and stroked her face, staring intently into her eyes. 'There's going to be a lot of pain but we will handle it together. You and me. I won't let them hurt you.'

'It's not me I'm worried about.'

'I know it isn't.' He brought his face close to hers. 'We'll get through this, okay?'

His lips brushed hers, a gentle, soothing caress that loosened a little of the anguish looping inside her at what they faced and the destruction they were going to cause.

Matteo's words of comfort helped a little but did nothing to ease the guilt that cramped her at what he was going through or the guilt at what she was keeping from him.

A loud cough from the other side of the room broke the moment.

The youngest of Matteo's chefs walked in carrying a tray with two plates covered in silver lids on it.

'Thanks, Leon,' Matteo said. 'Sorry to impose on your night off.'

'No worries. I'll hang around in case you need anything else.'

'If I need anything I'll get it for myself. Take a couple of hundred from petty cash and take your girlfriend out.'

Leon's face lit up. 'You're sure?'

'Sure I'm sure. Pay for any cab on the staff account.'

Leon saluted and scarpered before Matteo could change his mind.

'That was generous of you,' Natasha said, finding she could smile again.

'He was prepared to give up his night off. He's the generous one. Now let's see what we have.' He leaned over the table and lifted the lid off her plate and then the lid off his own to reveal plates heaped with thick-cut English-style chips and thick club sandwiches that managed to be artfully presented.

'You remembered,' she said in delight.

'I'm like an elephant.' He winked. 'In more ways than one. And eating here rather than by the docks guarantees your chips won't be stolen by seagulls.'

She couldn't help but laugh.

'That's better,' he said approvingly before his features became serious. 'I know it's going to be hard but there's no point in worrying about what's going to happen when we tell them. It's beyond our control. We'll deal with it when the time comes.'

Knowing he was right, she picked up her sandwich and bit into it. 'It's lovely,' she said when she'd swallowed the second bite down. And it *was* lovely. How could it not be? He employed world-class chefs who could make an ordinary sandwich taste as if it had been touched by magic. Everything he owned was the best.

A few minutes later Matteo had wolfed his plate clean and sat back lazily to watch her eat.

As if her eyes were magnets drawn to him, she was helpless to stop from staring back at him.

When she couldn't manage another bite she pushed her plate to one side and took a sip of the juice he'd poured for her.

'You've had enough?' he asked.

She nodded.

'Can I get you any dessert?'

'Can you cook?'

'No.' He grinned. 'I can get one of the local restaurants to deliver.'

She laughed. 'Honestly, I'm full.'

Just as he was about to lean in for another kiss, his phone vibrated across the shiny surface of the table.

Matteo debated ignoring it but knew he couldn't.

That's what came of having a business that spanned the globe, he thought ruefully, swiping to read the message that had come in. Your time was rarely your own.

Today had been an exception, one he felt he should make a regular thing. He rarely worked evenings but his days were always full.

'It's from Francesca,' he said, reading the message. 'She wants to know how I'm getting on with equipment and staffing levels for the hospital.' He rolled his eyes. 'I would have thought her new fiancé would have distracted her from ordering everyone around.'

Her answering grin showed she knew there was no malice behind his observation of his bossy cousin.

'How are you getting on with it?' As she asked, Natasha topped both their glasses up with more juice.

'I've ordered most of the equipment but I'm coming up short on the staff.' Matteo had promised to send his own medical staff to work there for a month to get the hospital up and running, giving them time to recruit permanent medical staff and train local Caballerons to do the auxiliary work.

'What are you going to do about it?'

'I don't know. I'm offering incentives but…'

'Nobody wants to work in such a dangerous country even if Aguadilla and the Dominican Republic are close enough to fly to,' she finished.

She scrunched her nose and looked at him. 'Did you really expect it to be any different?'

'What do you mean?'

'You employ doctors and nurses who've turned their backs on healing patients. They're hardly humanitarian sorts.'

'My staff *are* healers,' he refuted. 'They're dedicated professionals.'

'They're professionals,' she conceded. 'But if they ever had ideals they've traded them for money. Your clinics are specifically tailored for the filthy rich. Your surgeons are some of the top earning professionals in the world.'

He hated that she was right. He hated that she must put him in the same bracket. He hated that she was right to.

Like him, the surgeons he employed had paid their dues in the long years of their residencies. Like him, they and the other clinicians he employed had gone into medicine for noble reasons.

She tilted her head and narrowed her eyes as if she was thinking. 'What kind of incentives are you offering? More money, like Daniele's done with his construction staff?'

'Yes. I offered to double their salaries.'

'Forget the money. You want to go for their egos.'

'What do you mean?'

Although she'd only minutes ago declared herself full, she helped herself to a cold chip from her half-empty plate. 'Tell them there will be lots of media at the opening of the hospital like there is when you open a new clinic, and that there's a good chance they'll be interviewed about it and that the world will laud them for their self-sacrifice and humanity. I bet they'll rip your arm off to go there if they think they could make the cover of a magazine off the back of it.'

He shook his head and bit back a laugh. 'I can't believe I didn't think of that.'

'So you think that *could* work to incentivise them?' She looked rather stunned, as if she hadn't thought her idea would pass muster.

'It's a great idea. I've got lots of contacts in the media; we should get in touch with them and get some interest going.'

'I can do that. I did promise Francesca I would

take care of the publicity for it and until now I've barely thought about it.'

'I'll get a list together for you. I warn you, it's a long list so you might find it easier to work from my study.'

Her eyes widened. 'Really? You wouldn't mind me working in there?'

'Why should I? Most of my contacts are involved with the fashion and film industry side of the media so it's unlikely to interest them, but they should be able to give you other contacts to speak to about it.'

'Why are your contacts from the fashion and film world?'

'Because the people who come to my clinics and use my skincare range are generally people seeking to emulate what they see on the catwalk and the big screen, whether it's by buying a fifty-thousand-dollar handbag or making improvements to their skin.' He saw the flicker of distaste wrinkle her nose and added, 'That's not all we do, although I can appreciate why you would think it is. When I opened my first clinic I deliberately targeted that market, but the work we do, it's not all breast lifts and tummy tucks and people who want a new nose for cosmetic reasons. We also deal with cancer survivors; women who've had mastectomies and come to us because they know we'll reconstruct their breasts to look so natural that no one would know they weren't real, people who've lost half their noses because of a malignant mole…all sorts of people. It's not all vanity.

'But I do employ the best and I pay them accordingly and charge my clients accordingly for it. We've grown quickly and gained a reputation as the best for a reason—because we *are* the best at what we do. Yes, my staff have enormous egos but they earned them. They worked as hard as I did to become as skilled as they are now, and now they're reaping the rewards for all the dedication and commitment they gave for all those years.'

Her eyes never left his face while he explained the facts of the situation, delivered because of a compulsion for her to understand.

When he was done a wry smile played on her lips. 'I'm sorry if I came across as judgemental.'

'Don't be,' he urged. He took her hand and

kissed it. 'I meant what I said. Always be honest with me. Always tell me the truth. I don't know what's happening between us. I don't know if there ever will be an "us" in the real sense of the word but I know we owe it to ourselves and our child to explore it and see if it leads anywhere, but that can't happen unless we trust each other. I want to trust you, *bella*.'

'I trust *you*,' she admitted in a whisper, those vivid blue eyes huge. He thought he detected fear in them.

What did she have to be fearful about…?

'But what if it doesn't work?' she continued in that same low voice. 'What if the past—'

'Then we deal with it,' he said, cutting her off. 'The past is done. It's the future—our future, our baby's future—that matters. We can make a whole list of what-ifs but neither of us knows what the future holds.' He took a long breath, unable to believe he was having these thoughts and having this conversation with the woman he had so recently despised with every fibre of his being.

But he didn't hate her any more, and as he was the one demanding complete openness and honesty, he had to be honest with himself and admit that his feelings for her had consumed him since the day he'd first set eyes on her. One way or another, she had always been with him.

'Let's just take it a day at a time.'

'One day at a time?'

'One day at a time.'

Her answer was to shift onto his lap, wrap her arms around him and kiss him.

The most delicious swirling sensation was happening on Natasha's belly. It took a few moments to realise she wasn't in the middle of a dream.

Slowly she opened her eyes to find Matteo propped on an elbow looking at her and trailing his fingers over her naked stomach.

His lips curved into the sensual smile that made her heart skip before he leaned down to brush a kiss on her mouth.

'What time is it?' she asked sleepily. The sun was up but the light filtering into the bedroom was still hazy.

'Seven.'

'Shouldn't you be gone?' He had a full day of

surgery booked in at his clinic and then he was flying to Los Angeles to conduct interviews for a new general manager for one of his stores in the morning. He'd promised to be back in time to take her out to dinner tomorrow night.

In the week since they'd become lovers it would be the first time she'd slept without him.

In four days he would fly to Caballeros.

In five days they would be facing the music.

'I should, yes.' He brushed another kiss to her lips. 'Something much more important caught my attention.'

'Oh?'

He circled one of her breasts with his forefinger. 'I was looking at the changes the pregnancy's made to your body.'

'And?' She was barely three months but the changes were there.

'And they're beautiful.'

'Will you still think that when I'm waddling like a duck and covered in stretch marks?' she asked, trying to make her voice jokey, not wanting to admit her fear that the coming changes would be enough to turn him off her.

He rolled on top of her, his erection pressed right at the apex of her thighs, and gazed deep into her eyes. 'Whatever changes the pregnancy makes will only make you more beautiful. Do you know why?'

She shook her head.

'Because every stretch mark and all the other things that come with it will be visible proof of the life you've nurtured. And I'll tell you something else…' He slid inside her and with a groan said into her ear, 'You'll still be the most beautiful woman in my eyes.'

CHAPTER TEN

NATASHA'S PHONE RANG and she dived into her bag, which she'd laid by her feet, glad of the distraction.

In twenty minutes Matteo would be leaving to fly to Caballeros. She read the message and bit her lip.

'Who's that from?' he asked, leaning over and helping himself to a slice of toast from the spread that had been laid out for their breakfast.

'My mother. She wants to know if I've heard from Pieta's lawyers.' She fired a quick message back.

'Is she after money?'

'Probably. They're going to have a fit when I tell them I'm not taking any of it.'

'Are you still set on that?'

'More than ever. I spoke to the lawyer in charge and told him I want it to go to the foundation.'

'When was that?'

'Yesterday when you were at work.' He'd gone to New York for a day-long business meeting. Instead of staying in his Manhattan apartment he'd flown the six-hour round trip to be home in time for bed. 'Sorry, it was an impulsive thing. I never got the chance to mention it to you.'

He shrugged. 'I'm not your keeper, *bella*. So you want all the inheritance to go to the foundation?'

'Every penny. When I think how much work it's been this week for us to drum up press interest and change your staff's minds about working there for a month it brings home how important a healthy bank balance is for the foundation.'

The day after they'd become lovers, Matteo had come home from work with a printout of all his media contacts. Natasha had snatched at it, delighted to have something she could get stuck into for the long periods of time she was alone.

As he'd promised, Matteo set her up in his office so she could work. He even gave her the password for his computer. At first she'd sat in the office feeling like an intruder, her mind fleeing back to the day she'd returned from her brief honeymoon, already knowing she'd made the biggest mistake of her life. Her new husband had turned to her and said his study was his private space and off limits to her. She'd known throughout their long engagement that Pieta craved his privacy but to be excluded from a room of the house she was now supposed to call a home had been yet another kick in the teeth. She hadn't suspected then that the worst kick was still to come.

Matteo never made her feel like a nuisance. He never made her feel that she was intruding in his space. Living with him felt natural.

With increasing confidence, she'd made the calls. As Matteo had suspected, a memorial hospital being built in one of the most dangerous countries in the world was not something that interested his glamorous contacts in the media. However, they'd been generous enough to point her in the direction of editors at the more highbrow end of the media and they *had* been receptive to the idea of covering the story, expressing enough of an interest that Matteo had been able to send a memo to his clinical staff worldwide telling them of the media presence that would be in Caballeros. As a result, over two dozen surgeons and nurses had signed up to spend a month there when the hospital opened. It wasn't as large a number as they'd hoped for, but it would be enough.

It felt good to know that whatever happened between them and the Pellegrinis, they would have played their part in the memorial for Pieta.

'You knew that already surely?'

'The only involvement I had with the foundation was attending the fundraisers and press events with Pieta.' She'd offered to become more involved. If she couldn't work then she'd wanted to be able to do something useful but Pieta had always resisted. His reluctance for her to work had extended to his foundation and she'd had to wait until they'd married to discover why he'd been so loath for her to have any involvement in the running of it other than as an adornment on his arm when he required.

She dropped her phone back in her bag and looked at Matteo. For the first time in her life she lived with someone who made no demands on her or tried to bend her to his will. For the first time in her life she lived with someone who treated her as an equal and a person in her own right. For the first time she lived with someone who wanted to please *her.*

That didn't stop her heart thumping as she braced herself to say, 'I wanted to ask you a favour.'

'Sure.'

'You don't even know what it is yet,' she chided.

'I don't need to know.' He stood behind her chair and put his arms around her waist. She leaned back into him, thinking how right this felt. How right they felt.

'Your guesthouse, can I do it up?'

He stilled. Clearly it was the last thing he'd expected her to ask.

'Please? It's a brilliant space but it's crying out for the interior to be pulled up to the same high standard as in here.'

'And you want to do that?'

'Yes. If you'll let me.'

'How much do you want me to pay you?'

'Nothing. But if you like the end result, you can recommend me to your friends.'

He moved away to take the seat next to her and poured himself a black coffee. 'You want to work?'

'Yes. I want to do what I always said I would do and build my own interior design business.'

'What's brought this on?'

'You sound surprised.'

He looked bemused. 'As far as I'm aware, you've never worked. I thought you liked being free.'

'Well, I don't.' She knew where that idea had come from. Pieta. It's what he'd always said to justify keeping her shackled to him financially. And she, stupidly desperate to please, had let him. 'I always wanted to earn my own money but it was never an option for me. Our baby's due in six months. That gives me time to make a decent go of things. If it turns out that I'm not any good at it then so be it, at least I will have tried.'

'Why was working never an option for you?'

'Pieta wanted me to be available whenever he needed me. A career wasn't compatible with that.'

The bemusement fell from his face, his eyes fixed on hers with that look that always made her feel he was trying to read her mind. Which he probably was.

Eventually, his lips pursed together, he nodded. 'You are sure about this? You're ready to start building a career for yourself now?'

'Yes.'

'Then you have my support. Go ahead. Do the guesthouse up as you want.'

'That's it? No questions about what I want to do or if it fits in with your own vision for it?'

He shrugged. 'I got Daniele to design a guesthouse so I could have my privacy if I had guests stay. Other than that, I've no interest in it. I'll make you a signatory on one of my accounts so you can spend whatever you need on it and hire whatever tradespeople you need. Pay yourself a wage too. I've been thinking about setting you up with an allowance anyway...'

'I told you, I don't want to be paid for it and I certainly don't want an allowance from you.'

'Pieta gave you an allowance.'

'And it made me feel like a child being given pocket money in exchange for good behaviour.'

The longer she and Matteo were together, the closer they were becoming. There were times she simply ached to confide the truth to him. Matteo demanded honesty above everything else and knowing she was keeping something so fundamental about Pieta from him had settled like a permanent weight in her stomach. She had to keep reminding herself why it had to be like this when the doubts crowding in her head became too much. All she had to do was remember the devastation she'd felt when she'd learned the truth to stiffen her spine against confiding in him. However bad it had been for her, the truth would feel a thousand times worse for Matteo. He'd loved Pieta. They'd been as close as siblings.

But all this didn't mean she couldn't be honest about the rest of her marriage. Matteo deserved that much from her.

'Before we married I lived in an apartment bought in his name that was never mine. I'm sick of feeling that I'm living on handouts. I'm living under your roof and eating your food—

I haven't contributed a penny to anything since I've been here. Doing up the guesthouse for you is one small way that I can contribute and it also gives me the chance to cut my teeth on a project and see if the potential I was told I had at university is really there in me.'

Matteo swallowed back a boulder that had lodged in his throat.

Pieta hadn't wanted her to work. He'd given her an allowance that had made her feel like a child...

Pieta had been his cousin and his best friend but Matteo hadn't been blind to his faults. He'd been arrogant and aloof with an air of superiority born from being the eldest son of an old and noble family and knowing from the moment he could speak that one day it would all be his. But for all that, Matteo had always assumed Pieta would treat the woman he fell in love with like a princess.

He'd always been convinced Natasha's feelings for his cousin had been less than genuine, that it had been the money she'd been attracted to and not the man. It had made him furious to think of her playing with Pieta's emotions to her own advantage but had always assured himself that Pieta was a grown man. If Natasha didn't make his cousin happy he wouldn't be with her.

Now Matteo could see he'd got it all the wrong way round.

The question he should have been asking himself was whether Pieta had ever made *her* happy. Had he ever made Natasha feel like a princess?

It stabbed at his chest to suspect that the answer was no.

Matteo got out of the car and gazed at the shell of the hospital, astounded at the difference since his last visit there.

Daniele stood beside him and grinned. 'What do you think?'

He shook his head. When he'd last been here the site had been cleared and ground workers had been digging the foundations. Now there stood a sprawling building, unmistakably a hospital, complete with roof and windows. 'Has Francesca seen it?'

'Not in the flesh. I've been sending her updates and pictures of every stage.'

As Daniele spoke a tall, handsome man built like a brick wall strode towards them. Felipe Lorenzi, the security specialist originally hired to keep Francesca safe in this mostly lawless country and now designated the task of keeping Daniele's construction workers and soon Matteo's medical staff safe. He was also the man who'd captured Francesca's heart and would shortly be marrying into the family.

With a pang, Matteo wondered if he would be invited to the wedding. Or would he be cast out of their lives as his parents had cast him out of theirs.

He looked at his watch. Natasha would be boarding her flight to Pisa. In a few hours he would get back on his jet and meet her there. Daniele was taking his own jet back to Pisa too and had already offered a bet over whose pilot could get them there first. His cousin was oblivious to the destruction that was going to be rained down on them all the next day.

But now was not the time to be thinking of that.

He had the shell of a hospital to inspect and re-lated issues to discuss. He'd stolen Pieta's wife. He would not ruin his memorial too.

Francesca Pellegrini yawned widely and shoved the box she'd been packing to one side. In two days she would be moving from Pisa to Rome, into the beautiful house her fiancé had bought for them to live in.

He didn't waste time, she thought with a smile. When Felipe wanted something to happen, he was prepared to move mountains to achieve it.

Deciding to take a break before packing any-thing else, she made herself a coffee and un-locked her phone. One of her guilty pleasures was reading online gossip sites. Unbeknownst to Daniele and Matteo, it was how she'd been able to keep track of their love lives over the years. She preferred for them to think she was all-knowing.

The top stories were about the latest Hollywood divorce, which, being a huge film buff, interested her greatly. Before she could tap on it for more salacious details, a story lower down the page caught her eye.

Her finger hovered over the link for a moment before she took a deep breath and clicked it.

There wasn't much in the way of text, the story mostly comprising photos. The subjects were at a beachside café eating ice cream. The man's face was directly in the frame and unmistakably Matteo. He was leaning forward to wipe ice cream from the mouth of the woman he was with, whose face was mostly hidden from the camera's lens. The second picture showed him leaning in to kiss the part he'd just wiped.

Her blood chilling, she enlarged the first picture, trying to see the woman more clearly, even though her thumping heart already knew who she was. She would recognise that honey-blonde hair anywhere.

The teardrop diamond earring twinkling under the bright Miami sun was the clincher. Natasha had worn those very same earrings at Pieta's funeral.

After staring at the pictures for so long her eyes began to sting and blur, Francesca snapped into action.

'Daniele?' she said when he answered his

phone. 'I'm sending you a link. Prepare yourself. You're not going to like what you see.'

Only when Matteo was certain they'd inspected everything that could be inspected and discussed everything that could be discussed did he say they should call it a day.

As they were walking out of the hospital into the blazing Caballeron sun, Daniele paused to answer his phone.

'What?' he said, then took the phone from his ear and stared at it with a bemused expression. He looked at Felipe. 'Your fiancée is a complete drama queen.'

'Francesca?' Felipe asked, concern knotting his forehead.

'Do you have another fiancée?' Daniele jested. 'Oh, here's the mysterious link she thinks I need to prepare myself to look at.'

Watching Daniele open the link, a powerful sense of foreboding settled in Matteo's gut.

When he saw his cousin's eyes crease and dart to his face and then dart back to the screen in his hand, that foreboding deepened.

He just had time to register the darkest, ugliest expression he'd ever seen on Daniele's face before he was slammed into the wall.

Matteo had never been in a fight before but he kept himself fit and had reflexes that could put a boxer to shame. Pure survival instinct had him wrenching himself out of Daniele's stranglehold but the moment he was free, a flying fist connected with his cheek. He punched back, heard and felt the sound of crunching bone, pulled his elbow back to throw another but something as hard as granite attached itself like a vice to his wrist, rendering it immobile.

It was Felipe's hand.

Anyone else and Matteo would have been able to throw them off but Felipe was ex–Special Forces and knew how to use his body as both a weapon and a shield.

'What the hell are you two playing at?' he blazed before saying over his shoulder, 'If you take another step, Daniele, I will knock you out myself.'

But Daniele was already dusting himself down,

staring at Matteo with pure loathing, seemingly oblivious to the blood pouring from his nose.

Breathing heavily, trying to get air into his winded lungs, Matteo stared back at the man who'd treated him like a brother, and heard himself say, 'She's having my baby.'

Daniele took a step back, his face contorted, then raised his hand. 'Don't say another word. Don't ever speak to me again. You are no cousin of mine. You're dead to me.'

In silence, Matteo and Felipe, who'd released his hold on him, watched Daniele stagger away and into the car that was supposed to take them all back to airport.

After too long a time had passed, Felipe said quietly, 'I'll get one of my men to collect us.'

'Thank you,' he muttered. 'You should go back to Pisa too. Francesca will need you.'

A meaty hand slapped him on the back in what he guessed was supposed to be a gesture of comfort before Felipe walked away to make the call.

Matteo knew he deserved no comfort and with another twist in his gut he remembered that at that moment Natasha was on a flight to Pisa, ignorant that the explosions they'd expected to deal with tomorrow had already detonated.

The jet Matteo had chartered for Natasha lacked the personal touch of his private jet but was still beautifully apportioned and the cabin crew were all brilliant people who couldn't do enough for her.

So soothing did she find the flight that after a good lunch shortly after take-off, she found her eyes getting heavy and went to sleep. After a four-hour nap she woke to find a dozen missed calls from Matteo but no message.

Cold dread coiled in her belly.

She called him back but reached his own voice-mail and had to wait for an hour in nerve-shred-ding silence before her phone rang again.

'What's wrong?' she asked as soon as the phone was to her ear.

'They know about us.'

The line was terrible, the crackle of interfer-ence making it hard to hear. She put a finger to her other ear to try and drown out the back-ground noise of her own flight. *'What?'*

'They know. The paparazzi took a shot of us when we went for lunch at Miami Beach.'

She whistled lowly and rocked forward, coldness filling her head.

They couldn't know. Not like this. Oh, this was awful.

'Natasha?'

'I'm still here.' A loud burst of interference crackled over the line. 'Matteo?'

'Listen to me,' he said, his voice raised, his tone clipped. 'Wait for me at the airport. Don't go anywhere. I'll be landing soon after you. Just wait.'

And then the line went dead.

Scrambling through her phone, a quick search found the pictures Matteo must have been talking about. The headline would have made her laugh if she didn't think she was going to be sick. 'Dr Dishy Serves Icy Treat to New Love.'

Her name wasn't mentioned, which was one small mercy, and her face was mostly hidden. But anyone who knew her well would recognise her. Her family. Pieta's family. They would all know it was her smiling mouth Matteo was wiping the ice cream from and her lips he was kissing.

She'd known that telling Pieta's family would be difficult, especially the part about the pregnancy. She'd known it would be even more difficult for them to hear it. The last thing she'd wanted them to think was that she and Matteo had embarked on a carefree affair with no consideration for the man they'd just buried. These pictures... It could only be worse if they'd been pictured dancing on Pieta's grave.

If there had ever been any hope of forgiveness these pictures had ended it.

Natasha had bitten her nails as a child, a habit finally broken by her mother smearing strong mustard over them. If she had still been biting them then by the time her plane landed she was certain there would be nothing left of them.

They landed in the early morning, the sun only just waking in the frigid cloudless sky.

Coming from the balmy heat of Miami, the dramatic change in temperature was a shock to her system and she was glad of Matteo's reminder to take something warm to change into for her arrival.

Once she'd cleared security she found a seat with a good view of all arrivals and waited.

An hour later he appeared.

Covering her mouth in horror, she got to her feet.

Impeccably dressed as always, in a dark grey suit covered with a lamb's wool overcoat, it didn't detract from his red cheekbone and puffy eye.

She went straight into his arms and held him tightly before tilting her head to look at him more closely. 'What happened?'

'Daniele.'

She closed her eyes and buried her head in his chest, felt his own arms wrap around her and hold her just as tight. 'I'm so sorry,' she whispered.

'So am I.' He rested his mouth on the top of her head, his warm breath swirling through her hair. 'Did you see the pictures?'

'Yes. I had no idea they were being taken.'

'Neither did I.'

'Your poor face.'

Unwrapping his arms from her, he took her

face in his hands. 'It looks worse than it is. I think I've broken his nose.'

She turned her cheek to kiss his palm. 'Is he okay?'

'He will be.'

'What do we do now?'

'Now we go back to your house and get some sleep.' That had always been the plan. Natasha needed to pack the last of her stuff and deal with lawyers and all the other things needed to make a clean break.

'Shall we still go and see them later?'

His face tightened. 'Francesca messaged me. They don't want to see us.'

Her message had been emphatic, Matteo recalled, his lungs tightening.

He'd known from the second Natasha had appeared white-faced at the door with the pregnancy test in his hand that he was going to lose his family but he hadn't known how deeply the wound would cut...

He blinked, surprised at his own thoughts.

How had he known that when he'd managed to

convince himself for two weeks that the chances of him being the father were negligible?

But you did know. You knew in your heart that you were the father.

Kissing her mouth, he rubbed his nose to hers. 'We're both exhausted. Things will seem better once we've slept.'

Just having Natasha back in his arms already soothed a little of the pain.

CHAPTER ELEVEN

THE HOUSE HAD A COLD, unlived-in feeling that Matteo felt as soon as he closed the front door behind them.

Past the reception room, they went into the day room. The antique bureau in the corner was piled high with post.

'Are you okay?' he asked, rubbing Natasha's back. There had been visible apprehension on her face when they'd pulled up outside the house and now she seemed to have withdrawn into herself.

She looked at him and nodded, her smile rueful. 'It feels strange being back here.'

'Not what you expected?'

She rubbed her arms. 'It feels like I never lived here.' Then she blinked and seemingly snapped herself out of the melancholy. 'I'm going to make a hot chocolate before we go to bed. Do you want one?'

'Hot chocolate sounds good to me.'

She disappeared into the kitchen, leaving him to look around the gleamingly magnificent room. He recalled her saying once that everything here was Pieta's, remembered his own impression of the house that it had all seemed to match Pieta's personality.

There was nothing here of Natasha. His own house in Miami...it was like she'd imprinted herself into the walls. She fitted.

She didn't fit here. She didn't belong here.

This house was like a museum for antiquities.

He brushed his fingers over the surface of the bureau and as he wondered what century it was from, the postmark of the top envelope in the pile of post caught his eye.

Taking hold of it, he looked more closely, trying to comprehend why there should be a letter addressed to Mr and Mrs Pellegrini from Paris's leading fertility clinic. It was postmarked two days before Pieta's death, and from all the marks and stamps on it had been forwarded in recent weeks from Pieta's apartment in Paris.

'I hope you didn't want sugar added to yours,' she said, coming back into the room.

He spun round to find her carrying two steaming mugs, which she carefully placed on coasters on the antique coffee table.

'What's this?' he said.

'What's what?' She took the envelope from him, her hands stilling when she too noticed the postmark and the name of the clinic it had been sent from.

'Aren't you going to open it?'

She looked up at him, the colour draining from her face. There was definite apprehension in her eyes.

'Open the letter,' he commanded.

Still she didn't move, the apprehension now replaced with a hint of fear.

Snatching it from her hand, Matteo ripped the envelope open. Inside were two sheets of paper. He gave one sharp shake to unfurl them, and began to read.

He had to read them three times and even then it still didn't make sense.

'You were going to have fertility treatment?'

Her throat moved and her lips parted but no sound came out.

He held the first sheet up for her to see. 'This is a letter confirming an appointment in the New Year for you to begin fertility treatment and this...' he held the second sheet up '...is the confirmed price list. The letter also confirms that Pieta's sperm test results came back as normal.'

And still she didn't say anything, her eyes huge with an expression he recognised.

It had been the look she'd given him all that time ago when he'd asked the last time she and Pieta had been intimate together. It was the look she gave when she was trying to think of an answer when the truth should simply fall from her tongue.

He rubbed his hand over his head, trying to dull the thuds pounding in it. 'Why were you going the IVF route to conceive a child? This letter confirms Pieta's fertility and we both know you're fertile. You were only married for a year. Pieta himself told me you two only started trying after your wedding—that's too short a time to start thinking you might have fertility issues...'

He checked himself and blew a puff of air out. None of this made sense. None of it.

'Natasha, I need you to be honest with me. Why would a young married couple without any fertility issues like you and Pieta put yourselves through the quagmire that is IVF?'

Her features had clenched so tightly she looked as if she could snap.

'I can't tell you,' she whispered, her head shaking with increasing violence.

If she had simply turned around and said they had both been too impatient to try any longer without intervention he could have possibly accepted that. But she hadn't and her answer made his stomach lurch to his feet.

'If I mean anything to you, if our *child* means anything to you, then you *must*. I deserve to know the truth.'

The colour that had faded from her came back with a vengeance, staining her cheeks, but there was also a sudden calmness about her as if she'd decided to stop fighting the demons and confront them instead.

'If I tell you, you can't tell anyone.'

'What?'

'This is important. You have to promise me.'

A big warning light was flashing, telling him to drop it, telling him it wasn't too late to just stop this conversation and go to bed, that whatever had happened in her marriage to his cousin was none of his business.

But he couldn't listen to it. The nagging feeling about their marriage had become as loud as the siren playing and now, with the door to it prised open, all he needed was to push and the truth would be revealed.

'If that's what it takes to get the truth from you then, yes, I give you my word.'

She raised her chin and looked him square in the eyes. Then she cleared her throat and said, 'Pieta was gay.'

Matteo's first instinct was to laugh. It ripped out of him, echoing off the walls, and then soaked into the silence.

As if Pieta had been gay. It wasn't possible. He'd known him all his life, for thirty-five years. They'd been best friends, cousins, brothers... If

Pieta had been gay then the moon really was made of cheese.

Natasha hadn't moved. There wasn't the hint of a smile on her face.

His laughter died as abruptly as it had begun. 'You're lying.'

'No,' she said softly, compassion in her eyes and in her voice. 'I'm not. I'm sorry but *he* lied. To all of you. He was gay.'

'I don't believe you,' he said flatly. 'I don't know why you would tell such lies but it's—'

'I'm not lying,' she cut in. 'We couldn't conceive naturally. He couldn't do it with me.'

It was the way her voice caught when she said, *he couldn't do it with me* and the bleakness in her eyes that made him wonder…

No. She couldn't be telling the truth. He would have known.

Feeling his legs could collapse beneath him, he sank onto the nearest armchair and rubbed again at his head. 'If—and I'm not saying I believe you—but *if* Pieta was gay, why didn't he tell anyone? Why the charade of pretending to be something he's not?'

While Matteo could feel the fabric of his life crumbling around him, Natasha seemed to grow stronger, compassion almost glowing out of her skin.

'Because he knew from before he could talk that he had to marry. It was drilled into him his entire life. It was in the terms of the trust for the Pellegrini estate. You know what it says and it's been the same for hundreds of years—the eldest son inherits but only if he's married. He could never admit who he was. He didn't admit it to himself until he was in his early twenties. He'd been groomed since birth to be the heir and it was a responsibility he took very seriously.'

'And you knew this?'

She shook her head and slumped onto the armchair close to his. 'Not until we got married. He wanted to wait until our wedding before we became physical with each other. I thought he was old-fashioned...'

'Wait, you had no intimacy until you were *married*? You were engaged for six years.'

'We kissed but nothing more.'

'And that didn't set alarm bells ringing?'

'It should have done but, to be honest, it was a relief.' She grimaced. 'He was a gorgeous man but I never felt proper attraction to him, not like I always felt for you. I always hoped that when it came to it, something would switch on inside me. Maybe it would have. I don't know. I was a virgin. I didn't know what I should be feeling… well, I had an idea, of course I did, but… In the end it didn't matter. He couldn't do it.' She inhaled and looked at the ceiling. 'It was painful and embarrassing for both of us but more so for him. I was the first failure in his life.'

Not once in the past seven years had Matteo allowed himself to imagine them in bed together. Now he felt he could easily vomit.

His cousin, his best friend, had lied to him for ever.

And she had lied too.

Dio, after everything they had been through, she'd been lying to him when she knew how important honesty was to him, when she knew how hard it had been for him to trust her again.

'Why didn't you tell me?' he asked roughly.

Her eyes found his, her expression unwavering. 'I was protecting you.'

Anger bubbled like lava so strongly in his veins that he couldn't even speak.

She'd been protecting him? That was the excuse she was going to use to negate her lies?

She took a cushion and pressed it protectively to her belly, as if trying to muffle their voices from their developing child's ears. 'I had to keep the truth about him to myself. I knew it would devastate you. You, his mother, his siblings…you all loved him. Francesca idolised him. How do you think they would feel if they knew the truth?'

'What, that he was nothing but a liar?'

'Exactly that, yes. He kept the most fundamental part of himself a secret. If they learned that now…can you imagine it? If they learned he had never trusted them enough to tell them the truth about himself? When I learned the truth it almost destroyed me. I gave everything up for him. You. A career. Even my own thoughts. Everything I'd believed about him, all my hopes for the future… all destroyed. How could I put them through that? How could I put *you* through that?'

Matteo concentrated on breathing, refusing to look at her deceitful face a moment longer.

How did that old saying go? Fool me once, shame on you; fool me twice, shame on me.

Well, Natasha had fooled him twice. The first time he could forgive himself for.

This time he should have known better.

'Answer me this,' he said, keeping his voice under control by a hair's breadth. 'If Pieta *destroyed* you, why didn't you leave him?'

'Where would I have gone? Back to my parents who'd manipulated me into the mess? I had nowhere to go, no money, no job. He'd seen to that. He'd even sold my apartment so I couldn't go back there. I'd been in Pieta's power and at his beck and call for so long that I couldn't see a way out.'

Natasha closed her eyes. The pain and anger vibrating from Matteo tore at her heart. To learn the man he'd regarded as a brother had been a manipulative bastard and a liar could not be an easy thing to accept. This was everything she'd been trying to protect him from.

'Why the hell did you agree to have a baby

with him? Why agree to embark on something as physically painful as IVF for a man you hate?'

'He offered me a child in exchange for my freedom...'

'*What?* And you agreed to that?'

She could almost taste the disgust in his voice.

'No! Please, Matteo, I know you're upset...'

'Right now I am feeling many things but *upset* is not one of them.'

'I understand, I really do—I've been there. Why do you think I chose to keep it a secret? I didn't want to destroy your memories of him, especially when he's not here to justify or defend himself, but please, let me finish.'

'Go ahead. Finish your justification of how you would even *think* of bringing a baby into a relationship like that.'

'It took him months to make me even consider it. He made me many promises; that he would divorce me when the law allowed, that I would have primary custody, that he would buy a house for me and our baby to live in and put it in my name, all sorts of promises.'

'And you believed that after all the lies he'd already told you?' he sneered.

'Things changed between us. The truth being out in the open meant there was nothing left to hide. I knew I would never have another relationship—after what he'd done to me, how could I trust another man?—and I still wanted a baby, very much, so in the end I decided there could be no harm in going to the fertility clinic to discuss what it entailed. That was a week before he died.'

'So you *had* decided to go ahead with it.'

'No.' A wave of sadness flooded through her veins. 'When we got back to Pisa, he was so smug about it all. He took it to be a foregone conclusion that I'd agreed. I realised then that nothing had changed. He still thought he could manipulate me. I could never have trusted his promises.'

'How did he take it when you told him?'

'I never got the chance. The hurricane in Caballeros struck and he went into full-blown humanitarian mode, which for Pieta meant working around the clock with his foundation.' She looked at him, wishing he would meet her eyes. 'And I'm glad of it. I'm glad he died thinking we would have a baby together. I'm glad he died happy.'

With a sigh that could have been a groan, Matteo put his head back and closed his eyes, breathing heavily.

Sliding off the armchair, she knelt by him and put her hands on his thighs. His only reaction was to clench his jaw.

It hurt more than she could decipher to see the pain on his face.

Gently, wanting to take as much of the sting away as she could, she said, 'I know none of this is easy but he kept only one part of himself from you, nothing else. He was still a brilliant lawyer and humanitarian. He was still the man you played late-night poker with over a bottle of bourbon. He was still the man who supported you and was there for you when things became so intolerable in your home that you moved in with his family. Please, don't forget that. None of that was a lie.'

'Do *not* defend him to me.'

'I'm not.' She covered his hand that had clenched in a fist. 'He was a manipulative bastard but that doesn't take away the good things about him. It's not black and white. He was still human. In the end I came to feel sorry for him.'

His burst of laughter was guttural and bitter. 'He dangled you on a string for seven years and trapped you into a farce of a marriage and you felt sorry for him?'

'He trapped me, yes, but he was trapped too. He couldn't be with the man he loved. He'd trapped himself so tightly he could never be free to live his life as nature intended for him to live it.'

He moved his fist from under her hand and pressed his fingers into his forehead. 'I was your first, wasn't I?'

With a sigh she bowed her head. 'Yes.'

'A part of me knew that. I sensed it. I knew... I knew but I couldn't believe because I didn't see how it could be possible.' His fingers moved up to knead into his scalp, his knuckles white under the pressure. 'You let me believe he could be the father of our child.'

His eyes snapped open and met hers. There was a cold steeliness in them that sent shivers racing up her spine.

'I'm sorry,' she whispered.

"'I'm sorry,"' he mimicked. Then, before she could blink, his face twisted and he leapt to his feet. In quick strides he was at the fireplace where a row of antique English pottery sat on display. Swiping his arm across it, he sent them all smashing to the floor.

'*Sorry* does not make things all right,' he snarled. 'You have had weeks, *months,* to tell me the truth.'

Ripping an old oil painting off the wall, he slammed it on the bureau so hard it split, then swiped it over the large pile of post, sending envelopes fluttering in all directions.

'I never lied to you...'

'You were covering his deceit!'

'No, that wasn't it at all,' she implored, getting to her feet and holding onto the armchair to keep her shaking legs upright. She'd known he would react badly but it was still incredibly painful to witness his anguish. 'I wanted to tell you the truth, I really did, but I couldn't destroy your memories of him.'

'It's my memories of *you* that have been destroyed!' The lava in his veins erupting all over again, Matteo snatched a still full mug of hot chocolate and hurled it at the far wall. 'Everything we've shared has been a lie.'

'It hasn't,' she beseeched.

'You were a virgin! I have lived with the guilt of us making love on the night of his funeral, the guilt of you having my baby, the guilt of what our baby would do to my family... You have let me live with this guilt when you should have told me the truth after you'd done the pregnancy test...'

'I had a choice to make and I made the one I thought was right. I did what I thought was best...'

'You did what you thought was best for *you*, just as you've always done.'

'How can you *say* that? If I'd ever done what I thought was best for me I would have defied my parents and turned Pieta down. I would have married you.'

'Don't flatter yourself,' he scorned tightly. 'I would have seen through you before it ever got that far. You're a liar. You were a liar then and you're a liar now, but you're too clever to lie outright—you lie by omission because you're too spineless to tell the truth.'

She flinched as if he'd slapped her.

Matteo looked away, hating that his first instinct was to haul her into his arms and apologise.

How could he have been such a fool as to trust her again?

He took in the devastation he'd just wrought, the shattered pottery and crockery littering the floor, along with the dozens and dozens of unopened letters, the cream wall now splattered with hot chocolate, and felt as winded as he had when Daniele had slammed him into the hospital wall.

He staggered back and propped himself against the bureau.

'You're right,' she said, speaking softly but standing tall, breaking the silence shrouding them. 'I've always been spineless. I've always thought there was something wrong with me. I've never been able to please my parents—I always failed them in some way. I couldn't even make a cup of tea correctly, it was always too strong or too milky. I loved to ride horses when I was young. I won a gymkhana when I was eleven and do you know what they said? Not congratulations like any other parent would have, but that my posture had been off. It was all those little things that wrecked my confidence.

'Pieta was this brilliant man and I was in utter awe of him, and once I'd committed to marrying him I deferred to his wishes, just as I'd always deferred to my parents.' I let him dictate everything because I wanted to please him like I always wanted to please them. He *did* keep me dangling on a string but I have to face the fact that I let him. Then I discovered he was gay...' She sucked in a breath, looking as if she could be sick. 'What did that say about me? A gay man who didn't feel even a twinge of desire for me chose to marry me.'

'He chose you because you were a virgin and would have no one to compare him to,' Matteo said flatly.

'Yes. I see that now. I believe that now because of you.' She swallowed and made a move towards him, then checked herself midstep. 'You are the only person in the whole world who has ever made me feel that I'm good enough exactly as I am. I never thought I could trust another man after what Pieta did to me but there you were, where you'd always been, in my heart. You encourage me. You listen to me. You respect my opinions. You make me feel I could be anything I want to be. You let me be *me*.'

A tiny choking sound came from her throat, a tear spilling out of her eye, but she didn't seem to notice. 'I wish now that I'd told you the truth about Pieta and our marriage when the test came up as positive but I truly did think I was doing the right thing. I wasn't lying by omission. I was protecting you because you loved Pieta and I loved you. I've always loved you. I just wish it hadn't taken me so long to see it. I wish I could go back in time and phone you or email or send a carrier pigeon asking for your help when Pieta first proposed. I wish I'd had the courage then that I have now to fix the mess for myself without thinking I needed your help. I regret so many things but that one is my biggest.'

Matteo's listened to her justification with a chest that steadily compacted on itself and solidified. Almost as if they had a will of their own, his feet moved towards her and his hand reached out to touch her cheek. He brushed the tear away and brought his face close to hers, looking deep into her eyes so she would see as well as hear his every word.

'I understand why you chose Pieta over me,' he said quietly. 'I can see that I should have known from the way you kissed me in the *castello* that night that your feelings for me were true. I should have fought for you. I shouldn't have blocked you and cut all communication between us. I accept the blame I bear for that. It's been hard getting over my distrust and loathing of you these past few months but I did get past it and I learned to trust you again.'

A flare of hope flashed in her returning stare but quickly dampened to trepidation, as if she could read his mind and knew what he was about to say.

He brushed his thumb over her mouth, knowing it would be the last time he ever touched her lips. 'And that was my greatest mistake. I should never have trusted you. I have been living with guilt since our first night together and you could have stopped it. You have let me believe so many lies when you know I cannot bear lies.

'The only thing I have ever asked of you is honesty. You know how much I hated myself for the lies we were going to tell about our child's conception…you were going to make *me* a liar when, if you'd only told me the truth, we could have found a better, more truthful way. When I think of everything we've shared and to think you were keeping this from me…it makes me sick to my stomach. You had so many opportunities to confide in me but you chose not to. You made me trust you again. You chose to let me live with the guilt and for me to keep believing the lies until I dragged the truth out of you.'

'I wanted to tell you but I couldn't,' she whispered.

'What you wanted doesn't mean anything. It's what you did that counts. Your actions. You say you love me but I have to tell you, *bella*, you could say the sky was blue and I'd have to go outside to check for myself. I will never believe another word that falls from your pretty lips. My instincts to cut all communication with you back when you accepted Pieta's proposal have been proven right. I was a fool to trust you again.'

More hot tears fell down her cheek and spilled onto his thumb.

'It had been playing in my mind to ask you to marry me in the future but now I would rather marry the Medusa than spend another minute with you. The Medusa turned men into stone but you've turned my heart into it.'

'You don't mean that.' Her words were barely audible.

'Oh, but I do. The only contact I will ever want with you will be about our baby.' Dropping his hand from her face, unable to look at her another moment longer, he turned around and headed to the door.

He'd stepped outside—when had it become full daylight?—when she caught up with him and grabbed hold of his arm, forcing him round to face her.

'Don't tell me you're just going to walk away?' The tears that only moments ago had streamed like a waterfall down her face had been wiped away, although fresh tears still glistened.

They didn't spill, though.

'Were you not listening to me? Did I not explain myself clearly enough?'

'You explained yourself perfectly well but that doesn't mean you can just walk away. I've screwed up, I know I have, but we can get through this. What we have is too special to—'

'No, *bella*, what we *had* was special, but like your marriage it was a lie.'

'No, it wasn't and you can't pretend it was. I held back the truth about Pieta but I didn't lie to you. Everything we shared, you and me, that was real and you know it was. I love you and I know you have feelings for me too.' Another tear escaped but she didn't crumple. She kept her grip on his arm, her wet eyes boring at him. 'Please, Matteo, don't leave like this. Don't leave us.'

He had to force himself to remain unmoved. Natasha was the greatest liar he'd ever met. How could he believe anything she said or did again? 'Us?'

'We're having a baby…'

'You think I would leave our child?' he almost spat. 'Let me make this very clear, it's *you* I'm walking away from, not our baby. You should know better than anyone that I would never abandon my own child. I would never do what my parents did to me.'

'Then *stay*. Fight. I know you hate me right now but with a little time we *can* get through this. We're so good together. Our baby deserves to have both of us…'

'I agree.' Covering the hand holding his arm so tightly, he prised her fingers off, but before letting them go he brought his face down close to hers. 'And our baby *will* have both of us. But not together. I will never trust you again, and without that trust you and I have *nothing.*'

And then he let go of her fingers and walked down the steps to the path and to his waiting car.

'You let me go without a fight before, are you really going to do the same again?' she said, not shouting but with a timbre in her voice that made him pause.

He inhaled a breath and clicked his key fob.

'You say I'm spineless but you're the spineless one if you can walk away from something so special.'

He opened the door.

'Go, then.' Her voice had turned to steel with none of the softness his heart always melted for. 'But if you drive away now that's it for us. If you drive away now you can only come back for our child because I won't wait for you. If you're too spineless to stay and fight for us I will not put my life on hold for you. If you drive away then you and I are over for good.'

He got into the car and started the engine.

Numb to his core, he drove away. Before he turned out of her street, he looked in his rear-view mirror. The street was empty.

CHAPTER TWELVE

NATASHA SNATCHED UP her vibrating phone. When she saw it was her father, she didn't hesitate to decline the call. About to throw it back on the table, she stopped herself and took a deep breath.

She couldn't avoid her parents for ever. Between them they'd left over a dozen messages. If she didn't respond soon, they'd get a plane over to Pisa and turn up on her doorstep.

She spent a few minutes trying to get her brain to focus on what she needed to say and then composed a short message confirming that, yes, it was true she was pregnant and, yes, it was true the father of her child was Matteo Manaserro and not her late husband. No, she wouldn't be marrying Matteo. She signed off by confirming she would not be taking any monies from Pieta's estate.

Once the message was sent she breathed a sigh of relief.

Whatever she did next would be wrong in their eyes.

She'd spent twenty-five years trying to please them. Finally, she'd accepted she never would. And finally she found she no longer cared to try.

She wondered fleetingly if they would have the audacity to tap Matteo up for money. If they did she could well imagine the reception they would receive for their efforts.

Her phone vibrated again. This time it was one of the journalists she'd contacted about publicity for Pieta's memorial hospital in Caballeros. She declined the call, knowing she should just turn her phone off. The only people she wanted to hear from were the only ones who hadn't been in contact.

She wished they would, even if only to scream and shout at her. The silence was unbearable. Neither Vanessa nor Francesca would answer her calls. She'd gone to Vanessa's villa but had been turned away by the housekeeper.

Natasha's affair with Matteo was headline news

in Italy. The great Pieta Pellegrini's widow falling straight into the arms of his equally rich and famous cousin was too juicy a story to ignore. Luck had finally been on her side—they'd only discovered her identity the day after she'd moved into a new house. Three weeks later she and her new home remained off the media's radar.

Two days after Matteo had driven out of her life, she'd walked the streets of Pisa looking for a job and a cheap place to live. She hadn't wanted to stay in Pieta's house a day longer than necessary. It was the focus she'd needed to carry on. She had a child to think about and refused to cry and wallow in self-pity. What kind of example would that set? No, the only way she could help her situation was by taking control of it and setting out as she meant to go on.

She'd found herself a job in a coffee shop within an hour. She hadn't had as much luck with a cheap home but that problem had resolved itself when she'd returned to the house to find a note pushed through the front door and a set of keys.

It had been from Matteo.

In the space of two days he'd bought a house for her to live in. The note had made clear it was for their baby's benefit and not her own. When the baby was born he would put the deeds to it in its name. He'd also arranged regular maintenance payments effective immediately.

As much as her pride wanted to throw both the house and the maintenance back in his face, she'd resisted. Her baby deserved a decent place to live. Her new job would keep her going until the baby was born. She wouldn't spend a penny of the maintenance money on herself but her baby had a rich father and it wasn't fair to deprive it out of pride. She wouldn't take anything from him for her own benefit.

She'd hardened herself to him completely. If she was so disposable that he could walk away without a second thought, for a second time, then he didn't deserve her tears. That he visited her every night in her dreams was something she had no control over and something she refused to dwell on. It was safer that way. She needed to keep healthy, emotionally and physically, for her baby's sake. Their baby was their only reason for communication now, a few terse messages exchanged about appointments and scans and their baby's health. She knew she wouldn't see him again until the next scan in the new year. She stubbornly told herself that suited her fine.

But she couldn't harden herself to Vanessa and Francesca. Matteo had kept his promise and kept the truth about Pieta to himself so at least they'd been spared that truth.

Their reaction was nothing she hadn't prepared herself for but it still hurt. A small part of her had hoped they would forgive her. A large part of her still prayed they would.

She hoped they'd come to forgive Matteo too, then chided herself for thinking about him again.

And now, looking out onto the street from the dining room of the house paid for by his money and seeing Christmas lights twinkling from the houses across the road, knowing she was going to spend her first ever Christmas alone, she had to keep reminding herself why losing everyone she loved was for the best.

* * *

Matteo rummaged through the minibar of his hotel suite but couldn't find the brand of bourbon he preferred to drink.

About to put a call through to room service, he was interrupted by a knock on his door.

Wondering who the hell could be calling at this time of night, he walked the long length of the living area of his suite to the door. If the alcohol he'd consumed that night had done the job as well as he'd hoped, he'd be asleep by now.

He'd drunk steadily all night in the restaurant he'd taken his clinic staff in Florence to, their turn for him to grace their presence at their annual Christmas party. He'd seriously considered cancelling but knew it would result in a huge blow to morale. Tomorrow, Christmas Eve, he would fly to his apartment in New York and pretend to enjoy the festivities alone.

He couldn't even contemplate spending Christmas in Miami.

He was sick of travelling. He was sick of every place he visited reminding him in some way of Natasha, even countries that didn't have the slightest shred of a link with her. He was sick of the paparazzi following his every move.

From utilising the press shamelessly for publicity to promote his business, he now wanted to obliterate every journalist and paparazzo from the face of the earth.

He wished he'd been so lucky in obliterating Florence from the face of his schedule. Knowing Natasha was barely fifty miles away made it much harder to obliterate her from his mind. This was the city she'd had the scan in and he'd learned he really was going to be a father.

But he *had* already known it in his gut, his conscience insisted on reminding him. He'd known it from the second she'd appeared white-faced at the door with the positive pregnancy test in her hand, and had refused to acknowledge it for fear of what the truth would reveal.

He put his eye to the spy hole and stepped back in shock. Maybe the alcohol had worked better than he'd thought.

He took another look. No, there was his cousin Francesca and her fiancé, Felipe.

Apart from one phone call in which she had

called him every name under the sun, Francesca had cut him out of her life, just as Vanessa and Daniele had done. Was this the moment his hot-headed cousin had talked her fiancé into beating him up?

Taking a deep breath first, he pulled the door open a couple of inches.

There were no kicks to batter the door in and neither was there any of the expected acrimony on her face. After a moment of awkward silence, she gave a tentative smile. 'Can we come in?'

He pulled the door open to admit them, bracing himself for a punch in the ribs. But as they stepped into his suite he saw the puffy redness of her eyes.

'What's happened?' he asked, concern immediately filling him.

Felipe shut the door behind them as Francesca said, 'Haven't you seen the news today?'

'I've been avoiding the media.' No papers, no magazines and no internet. He didn't need to read the world's opinion of him. None of it could be worse than his own opinion, which had been getting steadily worse, although he couldn't understand why.

Blinking back tears, she handed him a newspaper that had been tucked under her arm.

He took it from her. Before he opened it he knew what it was going to say.

His instincts were right.

Pieta's secret was a secret no more.

'I'll get us all a drink,' Felipe murmured, while Francesca flopped onto the nearest armchair and wiped away a tear.

'Is it true?' she asked him, her eyes pleading with him to deny it, to say that Alberto, Pieta's right hand man for his foundation, the man now purporting to have been his secret lover for over ten years, was a liar.

He dimly recalled Natasha saying Pieta hadn't been free to be with the man he loved. At the time his head had been reeling too much with the magnitude of everything else she'd said to take that in too.

Taking the seat opposite Francesca, wishing he wasn't about to confirm something that was going to break her heart, he nodded.

'How…?'

'Natasha told me.' Just saying her name hurt.

Francesca's face went white as Felipe appeared at her side. She snatched the glass of liquid from his hand and downed it without looking at it or asking what it was.

She pulled the face of a woman with a burning throat then blew out a long puff of air. 'Oh, my God. She knew. Poor Natasha.' She began to cry in earnest. 'Why didn't he tell us? How could he keep such a thing secret? Did he think we wouldn't love him any more? Or didn't he love us enough to tell us? Didn't he trust us?' Then she leaned into Felipe, who'd handed Matteo a measure of Scotch too before squashing himself onto the single armchair with her, and sobbed into his chest.

Felipe's steady gaze met his. *No lies*, his look said.

There would be no lies from his lips.

It suddenly struck him that his promise to Natasha meant he was now guilty of lies by omission too.

He would have kept that secret without making the promise.

If Alberto hadn't sold his story, he would have taken Pieta's secret to the grave, not for his sake but for Francesca and Vanessa's. Just as Natasha would have done.

Some hours later, when Francesca and Felipe had left, Matteo sat slumped in his hotel room's armchair and stared at the thick carpet.

He'd never been as mentally drained or as emotionally shattered in his life.

But it wasn't the talk of all the secrets and lies his head was full of, it was Natasha.

She'd been with him every minute since he'd left her but saying her name out loud seemed to have opened a sluice in his brain and now he found she was all he could think of. He couldn't rid himself of the urge to call her.

He'd had this urge before, when Roberto had died, a need to hear the soft calming voice that had always had the power to make him feel better. He'd gone into medicine to heal people but in Natasha he'd found the one person who could heal *him*.

He dragged a hand over his face and fought for breath.

He'd thought everything was so clear but it wasn't. He'd been swimming in the fog and now the fog was clearing and his entire life was flashing before him like a reel playing in his head. The happy early childhood ripped apart by the fire, the withdrawal of his parents' affection, the guilt over his brother that had only eased when he'd found the one special person in his life who fully believed in him and who he'd refused to fight for...

Why had that been?

On and on it ran; qualifying as a surgeon, his brother's shame at his scars and refusal to leave the house, his brother's death, his father's venomous words and hatred, changing his name to spite him, creating his empire, every hollow success, Pieta's death, his child's conception, everything forging together into a circle bound by the soft glow of the woman he'd let back into his heart, the woman who'd sucked up all the guilt and fixed all his broken parts without him even realising…

He thought of Pieta and Alberto having to hide and deny their love.

Even if Pieta had found the courage needed to be open and grab the happiness that could have been theirs, death had taken it away from them.

It hit him like a punch in the gut. What he'd done. What his pride and terrified heart had done.

He too had had a chance of happiness.

Natasha had bared her heart and her soul to him and instead of embracing it he'd stamped on it.

She hadn't turned his heart into stone, she'd opened it and moved in.

And he'd thrown it blindly in her face without a backward glance.

Natasha switched the light on in the dark kitchen and filled the kettle. Her early shift at the coffee shop started in an hour and she needed to wake up.

Only a few weeks into her job and already she loved it. Right then, it was perfect for her. When the baby was born she intended to pursue interior design but for the time being this was just what she needed. It gave her the chance to be with people. She liked seeing shoppers pile into the shop laden with gifts for their loved ones. She liked the smiles, the little conversations conducted in her hesitant Italian, which over the last couple of weeks had suddenly improved by leaps and bounds. She liked the anonymity—if anyone recognised her from the press reports they would dismiss it as an uncanny likeness. She liked the constant smell of fresh coffee. She liked everything about it. She especially liked the reassurance that she wasn't alone in the world. That there *was* a world out there beyond her parents and the Pellegrinis. And Matteo...

Blinking his image away, she reached for a mug, then noticed her phone left on the counter overnight was flashing.

In amazement, she saw she had thirty-three missed calls, forty-nine text messages and over one hundred new emails.

What the heck was going on?

She scanned the missed calls first but there was no number she recognised. It was the same with the text messages until she came to one sent by Alberto.

What she read sent her reeling.

I'm sorry it had to be this way. I couldn't let them trash your reputation any longer. Forgive me for the pain I've caused you.

Gathering her hair together at the nape of her neck, Natasha struggled to control her breathing. She'd avoided all media since her name had been exposed but a quick scan of the internet told her what the apology was for.

She found she couldn't be surprised at what she read. Pieta had once drunkenly confessed to one great love in his life but had refused to name him.

It made sense of the pity she'd often detected in Alberto's eyes when he'd spoken to her through the years. It made sense of his weeping, 'I'm sorry,' when he'd clung to her as she'd said goodbye to him at the wake.

Oh, Alberto, what have you done?

Guilt at his and Pieta's treatment of her had led him to out himself and their relationship. Now the whole world knew.

Now Vanessa and Francesca must know too.

Her eyes fuzzy, her heart sad, she put the phone on the table. She didn't want to read any more. She didn't want to feel that if only she could bounce off the satellites that sent all these calls and messages she would find Matteo and he would make everything better.

Matteo had made his choice and he'd chosen to live without her.

And then the tears she'd blocked for over three weeks burst open again and she laid her head on the table and wept, crying for the love she'd lost, for the love her husband had never allowed to be free and open, and for all the hearts that were breaking.

It was the rap on the front door that cut through her tears.

She hadn't had a single visitor since she'd moved in.

CHAPTER THIRTEEN

APPREHENSION SLOWING HER DOWN, Natasha walked to the door, pulled the chains off then unlocked it and opened the door a crack.

And there he stood. Matteo. On her doorstep, a thin layer of snow falling onto his dark hair and long overcoat.

She pushed the door open wider.

For a long time, nothing was said.

All she could hear was the sound of her frantically beating heart. All her eyes could see was him, as beautifully handsome as he'd been when she'd last seen him. His eyes were bloodshot, though, she noticed. And he needed a shave.

She only just stopped her hand reaching out to touch his face.

Heat rising on her cheeks, the memory of how she'd once given in to the same impulse when he'd turned up at her door the night of their child's conception and then the fresher memory of how he'd cold-heartedly driven away all playing like a concerto in her head, she spun around and headed back to the kitchen.

'What do you want?' she asked, trying to keep her voice civil. However much she wanted to punch him in the face, she had to remember it was his child growing in her belly.

'To make sure you're okay. Have you seen the news?'

'Yes.' She sat herself at the table and looked at him, not inviting him to sit, making sure to keep her features stony and not betray the swirl of emotions rushing through her to see him again.

'Can I sit down?'

'If you want.'

He took the chair on the far side of the kitchen table to her and rubbed at his temples.

'Late night, was it?' she asked in as uninterested tone as she could muster.

'I haven't been to bed yet.'

'Been out partying?'

He sighed. 'No, I haven't been partying. Would you mind if I made myself a coffee?'

'Not at all.'

He pushed his chair back. 'Where is it?'

'I don't have any. I have decaffeinated tea or herbal tea. Knock yourself out.'

'You're not going to make this easy for me, are you?'

'Make what easy? Just tell me what you came here for then you can go on your merry way. There's a coffee shop round the corner you can get your caffeine fix from.'

Matteo had known this visit to Natasha's was going to be hard. After the way they'd parted he hadn't expected her to make things easy for him and he couldn't blame her for it.

She'd laid her heart bare for him and he'd walked away from her.

'I haven't been to bed because I've been up all night, talking to Francesca.'

'Francesca? You've seen her?'

He nodded.

The stoniness on her beautiful face softened a fraction. 'How is she? She knows?'

'She knows.' He closed his eyes. 'She's devastated, just as you said she'd be.'

'And Vanessa?'

'I haven't seen her yet but Francesca and Felipe came to me after they'd been with her.' He swallowed the bile that had lodged in his throat. 'She's in a bad way. They went back to her villa after they left me.'

'And Daniele?'

'I don't know about him. He could be with them too for all I know. I don't imagine he's in a better state than they are.'

She covered her face with her hands and pushed them up to brush through her hair. 'They must be going through hell.'

What could he say to that? Everything Natasha had predicted had come true. She'd known the truth would rip them apart and it had.

The man they'd loved and idolised all his life had not only lied about his sexuality but Alberto's exposé had revealed the truth about his marriage too. They knew their son and brother had married Natasha on a lie so he could inherit the estate he'd so badly wanted.

All their illusions had crumpled in the dust.

To his surprise, Matteo had found himself defending Pieta to Francesca. 'Remember how he was with you,' he'd told her gently. 'Remember the brother who was always there to give you advice and who encouraged you to fulfil your dreams when your parents were set on a different life for you. It isn't black and white. He was still a human and he still loved you.'

They had been so similar to the words Natasha had used to try and comfort him with that he'd almost choked saying them.

Natasha had kept silent about the lie to protect those she loved when, in truth, she'd been the one hurt the most by it. Pieta had lied to his family but it was Natasha he had lied to and used and diminished for seven years without an ounce of conscience. Matteo could have forgiven him for not confiding the truth about his sexuality—with distance he even understood why Pieta had felt the need to hide it—but he could never forgive him for what he'd done to Natasha. He'd stolen her life.

And he, Matteo, had condemned her for it.

Moving from his seat, he knelt before her, only now taking in the soft white robe she was wearing. She looked different from the last time he'd seen her. Fuller. She looked like a woman on the cusp of blooming with pregnancy.

Whether she would let him be there to witness the dazzling changes soon to come was something he couldn't guess. This was no longer the Natasha who had lived her life wishing only to please the people she loved. That Natasha was still there but with a tougher shell. She'd grown a steely resolve that he couldn't help but admire even though he knew it would make convincing her to take him back that much harder.

But he had to try. He'd let her go twice without fighting for her and if he didn't try now he would spend the rest of his life hating himself and filled with bitter regret.

He took the stiff hand that was on the table and wrapped his fingers around it.

She stilled, her jaw clenching, then inhaled deeply. She didn't look at him.

'When Francesca asked me if it was true about Pieta, I wanted so badly to lie to her and spare her the pain. I should never have condemned you for wanting to spare me and the others that pain, not for a second. I have been living with the truth for barely a month and it's been like a noose around my neck. You've been living with it for so long I can hardly believe it didn't crack out of you sooner. I condemned you for what I considered were your lies of omission when all along you were doing what you always do and protecting the people you love. You have the kindest, purest heart I have ever known and when you told me you loved me I should have got down on my knees as I am right now and thanked God himself for giving you to me.'

Her face changed slightly. The eyes that met his glistened, her breaths deepening, but her mouth stayed tightly pinched closed.

'Do you know what date it is? It's Christmas Eve. Exactly eight years ago I saw you for the first time and something happened in me…it was like you sang to me. I fell in love with you before I'd even heard your voice…'

Now her throat moved and she tried to pull her hand away but he clasped it gently with his other hand too, forming an envelope around it.

'You've always believed in me,' he continued,

knowing this was his one and only chance to make things right and that his entire future depended on his next words. 'You've always seen something good in me that no one else could see but I never allowed myself to believe it. It wasn't just my parents who couldn't forgive me for Roberto—I couldn't forgive myself. I knew in my head that the blame wasn't with me but my heart never accepted it, and in my heart I felt I didn't deserve happiness. It was easy to accept you chose Pieta over me when my own parents couldn't stand to be in a room with me, rather than trust in my heart and fight for you because, *bella*, the issue wasn't my trust in you but my trust in myself—can you understand that?

'If I had trusted my heart I would have fought for you but my demons wouldn't let me. There was a part of me that felt I didn't deserve the happiness I knew we would have together. I think I was waiting for you to prove yourself a liar this time round so I could justify to myself how right I was in cutting you off all those years ago because I was too blind to see and accept the truth, not about Pieta but about you and me.'

Her throat moved again and she inched her head forward a little. 'I don't want to hear any more,' she whispered. 'It's too late.'

His heart constricted. 'Maybe it is too late for us. I have to hope that it's not, but if it is then I will respect your decision but, please, let me finish what I came here to say. Let me have that and then I will leave.'

Her eyes closed and she inhaled deeply through her nose.

Sliding his hand around her neck, he pressed his forehead to hers and breathed in the scent of her warm skin. 'I knew something was wrong the night we first made love. I knew in my heart that I was your first but I refused to believe what every nerve and sense in my body was telling me. I was scared of what the truth would reveal, so you see, *bella*, I'm the one who's really guilty of lies by omission because I was too scared to confront what my heart had already told me was the truth.'

She was rigid in his arms.

His chest filling, he pressed his lips to her forehead. 'I'm sorry for hurting you. I'm sorry for every cruel word and deed. I'm sorry for abandoning you. I'm sorry for never fighting for you. I'm sorry for doubting you and for allowing my foolish pride and insecurities to blind me. I wish to God that I'd had the courage to believe in you as much as you believed and trusted in me and I wish I'd had the sense to admit my love for you before I threw it all away.' He found her lips and kissed them with the same clinging desperation she had kissed him with all that time ago in his office. He'd known then, in his heart, that she loved him but had been too blind and untrusting in himself to see it.

And now he had to accept that it was too late.

He breathed her scent in one last time. 'I love you, Natasha. Always know that. If you can never be mine again, know I will always be yours. I will wait for you, for ever if that's what it takes. My heart will always belong to you and the precious life you carry inside you.'

When he pulled away he found her eyes closed and her pale face taut.

He released his hold on her hands and gently stroked her cheek. 'Goodbye, *bella.*'

Natasha knew by the coldness that suddenly enveloped her that Matteo was walking away.

There was a lightness in her limbs and her head, a balloon filled with something undefinable expanding in her chest.

His words reverberated in her ears as his footsteps became more distant.

So many words. So much meaning behind them. So much love and tenderness and pain.

She opened her eyes.

Everything looked different. What had only minutes ago seemed dark was now filled with dazzling light, the surfaces of the kitchen units gleaming, the table she was sitting at shining.

And that dazzling brilliance was in her too.

She looked at the oven clock. She was going to be late for work, late for the job that had given her her pride and self-worth…

Matteo had already given her those things. She'd proved she could make it on her own. One day she might even be happy. But it was this wonderful man who had loved her and broken her heart who completed her and she knew with utter clarity that if she didn't swallow her new-found pride any future happiness would be stained. The bright colours evoked by his words now would fade to sepia. He was the one who brought colour to her life.

The balloon in her chest, which had been steadily growing bigger and bigger while Matteo had finally opened his heart, suddenly exploded and flooded her with the warmth she had never hoped to feel again.

He *did* love her. And he did trust her.

And then her mouth opened and she was screaming out his name, laughing and crying all at the same time, her unsteady legs racing to catch him.

But he caught her, in the small hallway by the front door, capturing her in his strong arms and holding her so tightly her feet left the floor.

'Don't you dare go,' she said, before finding his mouth and smothering it and his entire face with kisses. 'Don't you dare, don't you dare.'

It was a long time until he put her back down. He took her face in his hands and kissed her, before staring into her eyes, bewilderment and hope ringing from his. 'You want me to stay?'

She smiled her first real smile in so, so long. 'Only if you promise to stay for ever.'

The bleakness that had been etched on his face lifted, wonder taking its place. 'If you'll have me, I will stay with you for ever.'

She covered the hand palming her cheek. 'I will always be yours. I love you. I will always love you.'

He kissed her again, a kiss that conveyed more meaning than any words could. Into her mouth, he said, 'And I will always love you.'

With one final deep kiss, he lifted her into his arms and carried her up to the bedroom, where he proceeded to show her exactly how deep his love for her ran.

EPILOGUE

NATASHA STOOD UNDER the glorious late-summer sun at the entrance of the Pellegrini chapel at Castello Miniato and waited for the music that would cue her entrance to walk down the aisle. Holding tightly to her arm, as proud as punch to be the one giving her away, stood her brother-in-law Daniele, now the legal owner of the *castello* and who in approximately one hour would become her cousin by marriage.

Behind her, flapping the train of Natasha's wedding dress, was Francesca, taking her duties as chief bridesmaid with a little too much enthusiasm.

The music started and were it not for Francesca deliberately treading on the train to hold her back, Natasha would have galloped down the aisle. As far as she was concerned, she'd waited long enough to marry the man she loved, a man whose greatness had only increased in her eyes since he'd admitted his love for her. Matteo had sold his chain of vanity clinics to a hedge fund manager for an obscene amount of money.

When they returned from their honeymoon he would be opening a new type of clinic in Miami, a specialist hospital dedicated to performing surgery on the most severely disfigured people, adults and children alike. He would be funding the building and running costs and staff wages himself. It would be the first of what he planned to be many such specialist hospitals. Natasha would be in charge of the interior design, her brief to make it as homely and comforting as a hospital could be.

Forcing herself to walk sedately, she put one foot in front of the other and beamed her way towards Matteo. By his side stood Felipe, his best man, who, naturally, didn't look once at her as his eyes were too busy fixing on his wife. The Lorenzis had beaten them down the aisle by four months.

She smiled at her parents, sitting in the second row, and wondered if they'd asked Matteo for more money yet. She couldn't find it in her heart to hate them. They might be contenders for worst parents in the world, but they were *her* worst parents in the world and she looked on them as an example of how not to parent her own child. As she and Matteo lived in Miami and her parents were perpetually skint despite the regular large deposits Matteo transferred into their account, she rarely saw them. It was no loss, just as Matteo no longer felt the loss of his own parents. They'd created such a tight family unit of their own they had no need to wish for things that could never be.

The squeals of a bored, grumpy baby mingled with the music. Vanessa, sitting in the front row rocking baby Lauren, smiled when Natasha met her eye and blew her a kiss before attempting to soothe the fractious child.

Natasha blew a kiss back and then aimed one at her two-month-old daughter. As if by a miracle, the kiss landed and Lauren quietened. Or maybe it was Vanessa's magic touch.

Slowly the family had pulled back together, drawing comfort and understanding from each other. Natasha and Matteo had been pulled back into the bosom of the Pellegrini family too, and Francesca and Felipe had been delighted to accept the honour of being Lauren's godparents and guardians.

And then she was at Matteo's side and they were exchanging their vows and sliding on the rings that would cement their love and declare to the world that they did belong to each other and that no one and nothing could ever tear them apart again.

* * * * *

MILLS & BOON®
Large Print – January 2018

The Tycoon's Outrageous Proposal
Miranda Lee

Cipriani's Innocent Captive
Cathy Williams

Claiming His One-Night Baby
Michelle Smart

At the Ruthless Billionaire's Command
Carole Mortimer

Engaged for Her Enemy's Heir
Kate Hewitt

His Drakon Runaway Bride
Tara Pammi

The Throne He Must Take
Chantelle Shaw

A Proposal from the Crown Prince
Jessica Gilmore

Sarah and the Secret Sheikh
Michelle Douglas

Conveniently Engaged to the Boss
Ellie Darkins

Her New York Billionaire
Andrea Bolter

MILLS & BOON®
Large Print – February 2018

Claimed for the Leonelli Legacy
Lynne Graham

The Italian's Pregnant Prisoner
Maisey Yates

Buying His Bride of Convenience
Michelle Smart

The Tycoon's Marriage Deal
Melanie Milburne

Undone by the Billionaire Duke
Caitlin Crews

His Majesty's Temporary Bride
Annie West

Bound by the Millionaire's Ring
Dani Collins

Whisked Away by Her Sicilian Boss
Rebecca Winters

The Sheikh's Pregnant Bride
Jessica Gilmore

A Proposal from the Italian Count
Lucy Gordon

Claiming His Secret Royal Heir
Nina Milne

MILLS & BOON®

Why shop at millsandboon.co.uk?

Each year, thousands of romance readers find their perfect read at millsandboon.co.uk. That's because we're passionate about bringing you the very best romantic fiction. Here are some of the advantages of shopping at www.millsandboon.co.uk:

* **Get new books first**—you'll be able to buy your favourite books one month before they hit the shops

* **Get exclusive discounts**—you'll also be able to buy our specially created monthly collections, with up to 50% off the RRP

* **Find your favourite authors**—latest news, interviews and new releases for all your favourite authors and series on our website, plus ideas for what to try next

* **Join in**—once you've bought your favourite books, don't forget to register with us to rate, review and join in the discussions

Visit **www.millsandboon.co.uk**
for all this and more today!